BOOK ONE

THE DARK SECRET OF IAN'S PEAK

PARTS ONE AND TWO

ISBN: (hardback)   978-1-7638339-1-3
ISBN: (Paperback)   978-1-7638339-0-6
ISBN: (eBook)   978-1-7638339-2-0

Check out the website for more stories from Ian's Peak:

 +61 406 483 530
 www.djbrand.world
 admin@djbrand.world

Part One
The Experiment

Prologue

Strangers rarely pass through the town of Ian's Peak; when they do, the whole town knows about it. During the hot summer month of January, a stranger was passing through, while all the children were still on their Christmas break. Noticing no one was around, there was no motor vehicle or movement.

'Where is everyone?' he wondered, with little concern.

He was out to do a job and wouldn't leave until it was completed. The unknown stranger wore a black leather jacket, pants, and gloves and was tall with a solid build, someone you wouldn't like to meet in a dark passage. He walked through the town with only the sound of his footsteps. The high school he headed towards was becoming clearer in the distance. He remembered the school from his childhood. The memories that he was having for just a split second frightened the hell out of him, but deep down, he knew it would be all over in just a few seconds; he was holding a can of kerosene; this unknown figure seemed to be dangerous and looked quite angry at the world. He had planned to do something horrible and mad. The evil, tormented face said that he was up to no good, and that something terrible was going to happen tonight.

Lindsay Peterson had been the principal of Ian's Peak High School for twenty years, and he was also a former student. His fourteen-year-old daughter, Sam, attended the same school. This time of year was especially hectic for him, as he prepared for the upcoming school term. He diligently worked on the yearly planner to ensure everything was in order. Despite the school's challenges over the years, he managed well. A noise outside caught his attention, making him look up from his work. He saw shadows moving among the trees, which gave him an eerie feeling. He initially thought it was his imagination and returned to work.

This outlander of Ian's peak was standing outside the school grounds, and now he knew exactly what to do. A terrible memory, featuring the bastard principal, Mr. Peterson, invaded his mind, but he dismissed it almost as swiftly as it had arrived. The stranger picked up the can of kerosene and started pouring it around the school grounds.

Mr. Peterson smelled something burning and heard crackling fire nearby. Recognising the strong kerosene odour, he went to the window to investigate. To his horror, he saw a fire heading straight for him. He backed away from the window and tried to escape through the door, but it was too late. Flames consumed the school, and Mr. Peterson realised he would not survive.

The stranger disappeared into the night's shadow, waiting for the morning, as if he had never been there.

Chapter One

"James Thompson, it's time to get up," said the voice, that was disturbing my nightmare. My vision blurred, and everything faded: the school, the fire, Mr. Peterson, and even the stranger. Mary Thompson, in her nurse's uniform, was standing over me as I slowly opened my eyes. I took a couple of seconds to figure out my location, and then I saw the woman standing over me…

"Mum," I said, "what time is it?"

"It's almost nine o'clock," she replied. "You'll be late for work."

Like a typical teenager, I wasn't listening to Mum. I was still thinking about the dream I just had of Ian's Peak High School burning down and the death of Principal Peterson. The Principal found himself trapped within the building and couldn't get out in time. I felt the flames' heat and remembered the principals look when the devilish fire confronted him. That's impossible; it was only a dream. I had dreams like this before, only to find out that all the events in my dream came true. I remembered one dream I had only a few years ago, so clearly when Dad died. He was out chopping down trees for his work contract when suddenly, one of them fell back and landed right on top of him, killing him instantly. The night before that dreadful day, I had dreamed about it and tried to warn him not to go to work, and that something terrible was going to happen to him. He wouldn't listen to me and still went out and did what he had to do to support his family. Dad turned around to Mum that day, said the usual everyday goodbye and then to me as if he was going to see us again. Both my parents thought I was crazy, but I knew I wasn't. Things like that only happened since we discovered the laboratory that was hidden deep down in Cave Death.

I've never believed in the stories our parents told us when we were kids. A few years ago, I considered entering the cave during the school holidays. I was a curious ten-year-old, intrigued by the cave named as Cave Death. My best mate, Josh Brown, and I entered the cave together. I have known Josh all my life, and unlike me, he believed in the stories that were going around. It took me a long time to convince him otherwise. When I finally persuaded him to come along, he thought I was crazy. He didn't mention it back then, but we had been friends for such a long time that I could read him like a book; his expression said, 'Are you crazy? What if our parents find out?'

***

One fine Saturday morning, we were on the adventure of a lifetime. We rode our bikes up to the cave and parked beside it.

'It looks just like any other cave,' I thought.

I have never been this excited before. I jumped off my bike and quickly gathered my belongings together. Josh wasn't as excited as I was. When Josh arrived, he sat on his bike for a few seconds longer and stared at the cave. He didn't want to move any closer because of the legend that was going around.

"Do we have to?" Josh asked.

"Of course, we have to!" I said,

"But it looks so creepy," Josh replied.

"You're not going to chicken out on me now, are you?"

"What about the legend our parents warned us about?" Josh wanted to know.

"What did I tell you before?" I questioned,

"Our parents made up the legend because they didn't want us to enter the cave."

"Well, is that so bad?" Josh nervously asked.

"Look," I said, losing my patience. "Just get off that bike and follow me."

He knew he wouldn't win this argument, so like a follower, Josh got off his bike and gathered his belongings together. I was carrying a torch ready for when we entered the dark cave. I was in front of Josh for the entire journey and jumped over a big hole I saw on the ground. Josh wasn't so fortunate; he didn't see the hole, so he stepped onto it and fell into a giant pit. There was an enormous thump as he hit the bottom.

"JOSH!" I screamed while running to the edge of the hole. I looked down but couldn't see him anywhere because of the darkness.

"JOSH!" I called again, and this time, I heard a murmur that sounded like it was coming from far, far below into the darkness.

"Hang on, Josh," I called as loud as my lungs could carry, "I won't be long."

I thought we might need some rope for our journey, so I carried it across my shoulders. I eased the rope down the deep hole, tied the other end around the nearest tree stump, and slowly climbed down. When I reached the bottom, I turned on the torch to look around for Josh. He was lying on the ground, unaware of what had just happened. Josh tried to get up but couldn't because he'd sprained an ankle.

"Don't move," I said. "I'll see if I can find something to support you."

I shone the torch around and couldn't believe what I had just discovered: corridors in all directions.

"Wow," I said.

"What?" Josh asked; the pain that he was experiencing was just too much to handle.

"I think we are inside Cave Death."

"You're kidding."

"No, I'm not. Just wait here. I'm going to check it out," I said while walking toward the corridors.

"Okay, just don't be too long. This place gives me the creeps."

"I won't," I said, continued down the corridor and becoming increasingly excited about the discovery. I found a branch for Josh to use as a walking stick. At first, when he tried to get to his feet, he couldn't bear the pain; when he finally got to his feet, we strolled to the other side of the corridor. It felt as if we were walking for hours or even days. When we made it to the other side, Josh was ecstatic with the discovery that I'd come across. We found a strange-looking door with no handles and an inscription that read Dream Reality.

"I wonder what that means," I said.

We looked around for more clues to the inscription and a way of opening the door. I took out my notebook and wrote the inscription. Josh opened the door; there was a strange-looking button under a rock that he pushed. The door opened like an elevator. We saw what looked like a laboratory, as described by Mary

Shelley in her Frankenstein classic. There was a long rusty bench with buttons and levers.

"I wonder what happened here," Josh said with great curiosity.

"I'm not sure," I replied, "but I would love to find out."

We entered the room, and I went straight to the bench to inspect it. Josh wandered over to have a closer look at the buttons and levers. The machine looked so old and dusty, as if it had sat there for hundreds of years. I thought I would have some fun by lying down on the bench. There was a headpiece connected to the machine with wires. I put it on for my amusement.

"Hey, look at me," I said, "I'm Frankenstein's monster."

"Get off that thing," Josh said, concerned and worried. "You don't know how dangerous this thing could be."

"Relax, will you?" I uttered. "I know what I'm doing, and besides, this thing looks harmless enough."

"I don't know, James," Josh replied.

Straps attached to the bench that go around the body also caught my attention.

"Just strap me up, will you?" I said,

"I don't like this, James."

Josh strapped me down to the bench so I couldn't move.

I growled "Argh" like a monster, surprising Josh with my actions. His accidental backward movement knocked the lever, activating the machine. An electric current surged from the bench, jolting through my entire body. The shock I felt was so intense; it felt as if lightning had struck me and left me reeling. Josh's swift action to shut off the power in order to save my life resulted in the machine being turned off, but this took him a few seconds, which felt like an eternity. I was fortunate; the electricity died down almost as quickly as it begun. My body went limp, and for a minute, I thought I was dead. Then, I heard Josh's voice from a great distance.

"JAMES!" he screamed, "PLEASE, GOD, NO!"

I coughed and threw up on the ground. It felt like a truck had just hit me. An earthquake caused everything around us to collapse.

"Quick, James," Josh said, becoming frantic now. Josh unstrapped me, and I got to my feet, but they gave way, and I fell to the ground again. Josh helped me up. We grabbed our belongings and headed for the entrance and home. It took us a while before we found the entrance, but we found it. We were glad to see daylight again. When we made it as far away as possible, I couldn't stand any longer and fell to the ground in time to watch the cave collapse. I had a feeling this wouldn't be our last adventure, and I'm sure Josh was thinking the same thing.

"James Thompson, are you listening to me?"

I could hear Mum in the distance while coming out of the memory.

"What?" I replied.

"Oh, never mind, just get ready for work!"

During the holidays, I got a part-time job as a cleaner at Ian's Peak Hospital for extra money. My mobile phone rang for a few seconds; when I looked down, I could see that it was Sam Peterson, the principal's daughter, ringing me. I have a feeling that this phone call would confirm that I was right and that last night wasn't just a dream.

"Morning, Sam," I said.

"Hi, James," Sam replied. However, I couldn't help but notice the anxiety in her voice.

"What's wrong?" I finally asked, knowing deep down what she was going to say. I just refused to believe that I was right, and the dream wasn't just a dream.

There was no answer for a few seconds. Sam had never gone quiet on the phone before, not once that I could recall. At first, I thought it could be my mobile phone because I've lost reception a few times before.

"Are you still there?" I asked.

"Yeah, I'm here," she said. "It's Dad. He died last night. He was working late at the school when a fire broke out."

It was my turn to be quiet. Because I had witnessed the fire that killed Mr. Peterson as if I were in the same room, watching it unfold. I had a clear sense of what she was going to say and, considering the extraordinary nature of my experience, I actually was there in a way.

"James," she continued, "they said it was accidental death."

I can relate to how she felt. A few years ago, I was in her shoes when I lost my dad. I still don't know what to say to her, though. What could you say to your girlfriend when you have seen the whole thing in a dream, and there was nothing you could do about it? One thing I know, it was no accident, and someone had done it deliberately.

Why is this stranger coming into town doing this?

With a bit of luck, we'll find out the truth. How could I tell Sam I had a dream about it all happening while it was happening? She would think I've gone mad like my parents did.

"I'm sorry, Sam," I said. "Do you want me to come over today?"

"I thought you be working!"

"I'll tell Mum what happened. I'm sure she'll understand."

"That would be great, James."

"I'll see you outside the school grounds in half an hour."

"Sure, I'll see you then."

I pressed the red button on the phone to end the call and felt a creepy sensation as I looked around the empty room.

Why am I having another dream that feels real?

Is there a link between this and what happened in Cave Death all those years ago? Perhaps there's a connection somehow.

Chapter Two

Sam Peterson was waiting outside school when I arrived. Someone had vandalised the school grounds. Sam, a year younger than me and very popular at school, has been my girlfriend for over six months. She has long blonde hair, is slim, and have tanned complexion. As I headed to school, I couldn't believe my dream from last night had come true, and I couldn't even warn anyone; it could be my fault, when you think about it. When I saw Sam, she looked different. I knew she felt grief like I did when I lost my dad. I got off my bike, hugged her, and gave her a light kiss on the cheek. She relaxed in my arms.

"Oh, James," Sam said, bursting into tears. "Why did he have to work last night?"

"I know, Sam, but you can't turn back the clock."

"That's what I keep telling myself," she said. "He was in his office when the fire started. They found evidence it was arson."

"Let's go for a walk," I said, taking Sam's hand. "There's something I need to tell you."

"What?" Sam asked.

"Let's sit down."

We sat on the bench when I saw Josh. I waved to get his attention. He entered the cave with me years ago, but I never told him about my powers from the experiment. It's time he knew. Josh is taller than me, and he enjoys gaming online and browsing the internet. He came over to join us.

"Did you see the school?" Josh asked, noticing Sam looked upset. "What's wrong?"

"Her dad died last night," I said. "He was working late when the fire started."

"Oh, Sam, I'm sorry."

"It's okay, Josh," Sam replied. "You didn't know."

"What did you want to tell me?" Sam asked.

"We can talk later if you'd prefer privacy," Josh offered.

"There's something I was meaning to tell both of you for such a long time," I said.

"Well?" Sam asked, feeling more anxious than ever.

"I had a dream about a school fire last night," I explained. "I felt like I was there."

"What?" she asked. "Was my Dad part of the dream?"

"Yes, like you said, he was working late," I replied. "A noise drew him to the window. He saw the fire's approaching. He couldn't have prevented it."

"James, it's only a dream; it couldn't be real," Josh said.

"I've been trying to convince myself of that this morning," I replied, "but Sam's call confirmed what I already knew."

"What do you mean?" Sam asked curiously.

"A stranger, who I've never seen before, deliberately lit fire to the school."

"How is it possible for you to have extraordinary dreams like this?" Sam asked curiously.

"This wasn't my only dream to come true." I said.

"What other dreams did you have?" Sam inquired.

"I dreamt about my dad's accident the night before he was killed, and attempt to warn him the next day, but he wouldn't listen and went to work, that was the last time I saw him alive."

I felt disturbed about what had happened last night and started pacing around. Sam came up behind me and put her arms around my waist to give me a slight hug.

"You seem worried," she remarked.

"Josh, do you remember when we entered Cave Death few years ago?" I asked.

"The cave with a legend to warn kids not to enter," Josh replied. "but, we entered anyway; yeah, how could I forget?"

"We entered a room that looked like a laboratory set from a horror movie. I laid down on this strange-looking bench, and you activated the machine by accident. The machine electrocuted me badly!"

"I'm still not seeing the connection; what's that got to do with the dream you had last night?" Josh asked, looking confused.

"Well, I studied the history of Ian's Peak a few months ago and found out something interesting about Cave Death."

"What did you find out?" Josh asked, sounding eager.

"Historical records indicate that Professor Lynx performed a series of unusual experiments, known as 'Dream Reality,' in a cave during the 19th century."

"Are you trying to tell us that you were caught up in this experiment?" Sam asked curiously.

"Yeah, sounds a little bit far fetch, doesn't it." I replied.

"Okay, lets put all that aside for a minute, what happened in the dream you had last night?" Sam wanted to know.

"Someone came to the school, poured kerosene all over, and lit a match. Before you knew it, the entire school went up in smoke."

"Did you get a good look at him?" Josh asked.

"Yeah, he's enough to give anyone nightmares, the very thought of him makes my skin crawl."

"Can you assist the police by describing the man?" Josh wondered.

"Are you kidding? They would want to know how I got that information, and would make me feel like a suspect."

"James's right," Sam said. "the police would think he's crazy if he told them the truth. We have to deal with it ourselves."

"What are you talking about?" I wanted to know.

"We need to identify this stranger; once we have a good description and any other relevant details, we'll notify the authorities." Sam stated.

I replied, "No, it's too dangerous."

"He must pay for his actions," said Sam.

"Leave it to the police." I replied.

"With no description, the police are clueless about where to begin their search."

"Sam's right." Josh said.

I looked at Josh and Sam. Sam had a look, a pleading look, a look I couldn't resist for the life of me.

"Okay." I finally agreed.

"Great, I knew you would help." Sam said, giving me a slight hug.

I was wondering if I was working for Sam to find her dad's killer or for myself to find out more about the 'Dream Reality' experiment. I was thinking about it for the rest of the night until I fell into a deep sleep.

Chapter Three

The stranger has returned to the small town of Ian's Peak, driving around the streets, taking all the back roads in his silver Commodore, so no residents could see him. He parked his car in a good hiding place, where no one would ever think to look. The stranger left his car and set off on foot for the park, two miles away; the rhythmic thud of his footsteps his only companion.

That park kept haunting his memory. Children in the past used to gather at the park and play the evil game of football.

"Only sinners play football!" He remembered his mum bellowing out.

"These kids are sinners and will never make it to heaven because of the evil game they are playing!"

The stranger didn't come back to Ian's Peak years later to preach about football. He was here for revenge on something he remembered that had happened more than a decade ago. At the park, the stranger saw Josh Brown and felt a jolt of recognition; the boy was the spitting image of his father, Jack, even to the same unruly brown hair. The other kid, who is younger than Josh, is his brother, Paul. For a couple of days, the stranger has been watching Paul. He's going to get his revenge on Jack by taking something that belonged to him. Jack had taken something from him as a child, like his sanity, his girl, and his life. The stranger *was waiting to pick the right moment before he makes his move. He couldn't believe his luck. The football came right up to where he was standing. Josh had kicked the ball out of range; and Paul was running right behind it, and noticed someone standing there when he was about to pick it up. Paul looked up at the man standing only a few feet away, someone he'd never seen around town before. The stranger bent down and picked up the ball for Paul.*

"Hi, kid," the stranger greeted the youngster.

"Who are you?" Paul wondered.

Observing Josh from a distance, the stranger saw he was speaking with a girl who had long blonde hair. With Josh out of sight, the stranger didn't waste any time and put his plan into action.

The stranger said, "I'm an old friend of your dad. I'm in town for a few days on business, and your dad asked me to come and pick you up."

"Why's that?" Paul wondered.

"Your mum is very sick," the stranger said, "and he needs you home as soon as possible."

The stranger noticed Josh had gone further down the road with this girl he was talking to earlier.

"What about Josh?" Paul inquired.

"Josh has already gone. I have just seen him leave." The stranger's eyes flickered as he lied, his voice tight.

Paul looked back and couldn't see Josh anywhere.

Could this stranger be telling the truth?

Is mum really sick?

Why did Josh leave him all alone?

"Okay," Paul said.

"Good boy," the stranger said with a smile.

With the blonde-haired girl gone, Josh reappeared, his voice echoing as he shouted Paul's name. He was just a few seconds too late; Paul was already gone. Upon noticing that his younger sibling was absent, he immediately ran to the location where he had last kicked the ball. He found the football; Paul was missing. Josh cried out.

The buzzer went off. Everything in my dream came to a halt and faded before my eyes, and I was returning to reality again.

Another nightmare. I was dripping with sweat. With a quick movement, I retrieved my towel from its place in the side cupboard and wiped the sweat from my forehead. My mind wasn't clear initially, and then I remembered the dream. It came to me slowly at first, but eventually, in the complete picture. I turned off my alarm and looked at it for just a few more seconds. It had just turned eight in the morning. I still saw the stranger who abducted Paul.

'Josh, I must warn him—if I'm not too late.'

Reaching over to the nightstand next to my bed, I picked up my phone, intending to call Josh. As I touched the phone, a new vision appeared of Josh and his brother walking to the park. Josh left his phone on his bed, so calling him was pointless. Because of my unsuccessful attempts at contacting on Josh's mobile, I dialed their landline number, hoping to make contact. I could hear the ringing of their phone through my mobile.

'Come on, Josh,' I said to myself, 'answer the goddamn phone.'

Someone answered the phone; it was Josh's mum, Anne Brown. She sounded as if she had just woken up.

"Hello, Brown residence," she said.

"Hello, Mrs. Brown, this is James. Is Josh Home"

"No, I'm sorry. He already left, James," Anne said. "Josh has taken Paul to the park."

"Thanks," I said. "I see him there."

"Did you try calling his mobile?" Anne asked.

"No," I answered; "it was left on his bed, and he forgot to take it."

"Okay" she said as she hung up the phone.

'It was left on his bed.' Anne thought, 'How on Earth did he know that.'

I ended the call by pressing the red button. Paul's in trouble. I must inform them of a potential danger. I hope it's not too late. I took the back way to the park.

***

Paul successfully caught the ball after Josh kicked it towards him. He possesses a surprising level of skill in football, especially given his age; Having received the ball from Paul's kick, Josh kicked it back again, but his attention was so thoroughly diverted that he failed to notice the ball's destination and the extent of its travel. Josh was too interested in a girl at the park. Susan McGregor, a blonde-haired girl who had recently moved from Scotland just a few months ago, that he failed to notice anything else. Josh had always wanted to ask her out ever since she moved to Ian's Peak, but he was too shy to take the chance. He was quite surprised to learn she knew about him, because until today he had assumed she didn't even know he existed.

Immediately following another kick of the football, Josh ceased his activity and chatted with Susan. Playing football with his brother at the park slipped his mind.

While riding down the street, I was yelling and waving my arms; Josh saw me from the sidewalk but couldn't comprehend the meaning behind my frantic display. Curious about what I wanted, Josh cautiously moved a short distance closer to get a better look. Not knowing what was happening with Paul, I brought my bicycle to a stop, positioning it as near to Josh as I could while concentrating on slowing my breathing and regaining my breath.

"Don't leave Paul alone!" I cried out urgently.

"What?" Worried, Josh wanted to understand my unexpected outburst.

"Just trust me," I said. "Where's Paul?"

"He's over there," Josh replied, pointing in the direction where Paul was a few minutes ago, but realised he was nowhere in sight and started running in that direction. I jumped off my bike and ran after Josh. Josh found only the football, and Paul was nowhere nearby. When we couldn't find young Paul, Josh fell to the ground and screamed with rage. I knelt beside him.

"That's what I've been trying to tell you," I said. "I had another dream last night. I think it could be the same guy who burnt down the school."

"What am I going to do?" Josh wanted to know.

I couldn't answer him immediately, but deep down, I knew I couldn't answer him at all.

"My parents going to kill me!" Josh said.

"I'm sure it won't be as bad as all that."

"You want a bet? Dad went nuts for losing his best golf ball," Josh said. "You think he's going to pat me on the back for losing his son?"

"I guess not," I replied. "Come on, we better let your dad know."

Chapter Four

"YOU WHAT?" Jack demanded, while his face was burning red with anger.

"We were playing football," Josh explained, "then paul just vanished."

"He couldn't vanish into thin air!" his furious father retorted, his whole body trembling with rage. Josh and I were waiting for him to explode. Anne was sitting in the lounge, trying to calm down, but it wasn't easy.

"Calm down." She said.

"CALM DOWN!" he exclaimed, his voice tight with barely controlled fury. "Our young son is out there with some lunatic, and you said calm down?"

"It isn't good blaming anyone." She said.

I looked into Josh's eyes; he had a look of anger, desperation, and hate building up. He retreated to his bedroom, carefully not showing his distress over the situation.

"Look, Mr. Brown," I said, "I was there, and it wasn't Josh's fault."

Jack had to sit down; everything seemed too much in one day.

"I know where Paul was last seen," I said, "which could help us find him."

"James's got a point," Anne said. "Why don't you both go to the park and look around?"

"Okay," Jack finally agreed, "then I better speak to Officer Butler."

Arriving at the park, we searched for clues related to Paul's disappearance. Despite our lack of luck, my Dream Reality abilities helped me recall the car's hidden location before Paul vanished. I went straight to the spot where I remember from my dream, and found clues showing a car had been parked there, in a place nobody would expect.

"Look at this!" I called out to Jack, the sound echoing through the trees, and Jack immediately came running to see what I'd found. There were visible tire tracks in the ground. Touching the marks caused a flashback: a silver Commodore, the car from my dream. My eyes caught the license plate number, XLV221.

"The car is a silver Commodore, its license plate number XLV221." I said..

"How did you know that?"

"I can't explain right now. You need to call the police."

Jack took out his mobile and dialed the number for Ian's Peak police department. He waited a few seconds before someone answered.

"Yes," Jack said, "could I speak to Officer Butler?"

Officer Bill Butler had a twenty-year career with the Ian's Peak police department. Having known Jack since his teenage years, he was well aware of Jack's continuous brushes with the law, a pattern that only ceased after the timely intervention of Officer Butler. Jack recalled an incident from high school involving another teenager, a student who was later placed in institutional care. Bill Butler, the officer assigned to the night shift, received a call that evening requiring his immediate attention at the local school. Brown's record showed he'd be responsible. He left school in year ten without graduating. Jack and Anne named their newborn son Joshua a year after the incident. Jack found a stable job. His life took a positive turn, as he could then support his family financially and provide them with a better future. When Josh was born, dramatically altered Jack's life, transforming his personality from a less responsible person into a more mature and sensible young man.

"This is Officer Butler," the voice said on the phone.

"It's Jack, Bill."

"Jack," the officer inquired, "what's wrong?"

"Paul had vanished." Jack responded.

"Vanished? What do you mean by that?" Bill questioned.

"While Josh was playing football with Paul in the park, he vanished the minute Josh's back was turned."

"Where are you now?"

"I'm over at the park," Jack replied.

"I'll meet you there, and we might need to organise a search party."

"Great, Bill. There is another thing. I think he's been abducted."

"Are you sure?" Bill asked.

"We found evidence," Jack said. "James seem to remember seeing a silver Commodore in the area with a license plate number XLV 221."

"Okay, I check it out, and I can be at the park in ten minutes."

Jack hung up the mobile, leaving Bill with the information I had initially given him. Something else disturbed me.

Something doesn't feel right. I had a quick flashback. Whatever it was, took place a long time ago. The vision vanished from my mind as rapidly as it appeared. Concern and curiosity were clear in Jack's gaze as he looked at me.

"Are you okay?" Jack asked,

"What?"

"What happened?" Jack wondered,

"Nothing!" I replied.

Jack wasn't sure it was nothing. He knew something had happened to me. I didn't seem to be myself today. What happened all those years ago?

***

Officer Butler organised a team of guys to search for Paul. Jack had known most of them since high school, and they were as concerned about this happening to Paul as Jack was. No one had ever abducted a child in this town before. Why now?

Nobody seemed to know the answer.

While waiting to receive a phone call about the owner of the car, Officer Butler spent the afternoon in the company of Jack and Anne. After Paul's surprising disappearance, Bill talked to Josh and me again to figure out what had happened. All the information we gave him, he already knew. The only thing I kept from him was the fact that I had been a subject in a scientific experiment which gave me the power of precognition, meaning I can foresee the future, a phenomenon I call Dream Reality. I was very concerned that people would think I've lost my mind.

Never had Ian's Peak witnessed such a massive search party. The entire town was assisting in the search. They combed the area, hoping to find Paul. Sam came over to spend some time with Josh and me, keeping us company. Sam was still upset because of what happened to her dad and the school two nights ago. Once Officer Butler was gone for the day, the dream I'd had that morning stuck with me. Why was I delayed in getting there? I automatically assumed it was all my fault and kept reminding myself to stop talking nonsense. I warned Josh, but it was already too late. I left Josh and Sam and joined the search party. I suggested to Josh he shouldn't come and thought Sam might stay with him for company.

We looked for Paul everywhere. Including houses, sheds, areas behind shops, and bushlands. I haven't got a single clue where he could be. Why isn't the Dream Reality working when I want it to?

****

"They have searched for hours," Josh said. "Why haven't they found anything yet?"

"Don't worry, they will," Sam replied.

"You don't suppose he could be …" Josh said, but couldn't finish the sentence. Sam knew exactly what he was talking about.

"No, of course not," she assured him.

"I can't help thinking it's all my fault. If anything happens to him, I'll never forgive myself."

"Look, it's nobody's fault except for the person who abducted him," Sam said. "Why don't you get some sleep? You might feel better when you wake up."

"I doubt it."

***

Officer Butler suspected Paul was no longer in Ian's Peak, but didn't like to say anything to Jack. We searched everywhere, but there was still no sign. No one will give in and assured the family that the search would continue until they find something.

"Find something? What do they mean, find something?" Josh wondering, "Are they expecting to find his body?"

Despite my repeated attempts to encourage him to maintain a positive outlook, my words seemed to have no impact on him whatsoever. Unable to shake the horrifying image of his brother's small body lying in a coffin, Josh forcefully dismissed the vision from his mind.

Chapter Five

The morning was very slow for Anne; she couldn't sleep a wink. On this sultry night, the mother's thoughts turned to her son, her anxiety growing with every passing moment and the dreadful possibilities for what might have happened to him in the night. Because the idea was so upsetting, she attempted to distract herself from the thought, worried that she would have an emotional collapse that would cause her to cry. Who would do this?

Her questions went unanswered. Outside, a stranger in black, wearing gloves, approached the Browns' letter box, dropped an envelope in, and quickly left. Later that day, Jack checked the mail and notice the hand-delivered letter. Anne waited in the lounge. Jack's wife noticed his concern as he entered the lounge.

"What's wrong?" Anne asked with concern.

"This letter," Jack said. "It was hand-delivered."

"By whom?"

"I don't know," he said, opening the envelope. After reading it, he collapsed into a chair.

"What is it?" she asked. Jack handed her the letter.

"Your son is here today, gone tomorrow," she read. "Oh, Jack." She burst into tears.

"Don't worry," Jack said, comforting his wife. "We'll give this to Bill immediately."

"What if it's too late?" Anne questioned.

"Stop thinking like that," he said.

"We need to be realistic," she replied. "We may never see our boy again."

"Don't do this to yourself."

Jack examined the letter again. Something about it seemed familiar. What could the connection be?

Lost in thought, he recalled a memory from a time when he was the same age as Josh.

'Your son is here today, gone tomorrow.'

Years earlier, Mary had made a similar comment. In high school, she dated a boy who betrayed and murdered his baby brother, like the story of Cain and Abel. It's remarkable how closely that boy's words resemble those in this letter.

Mary told Jack, "Your brother is here today, gone tomorrow," recalling a past event.

The phone rang suddenly, startling Anne and Jack. He stared at it in the corner cabinet before answering.

"Hello," Jack said.

"Jack, it's Bill. I have news about the car's owner."

"Who owned the car?"

"It's not going to sit well with you."

"Just tell me."

"Someone by the name of Morton, Wayne Morton owned the car."

"We don't know any Wayne Morton."

"I did more checking. Morton isn't his real name; it's Wayne Cassidy."

"My God!" Jack exclaimed.

"Jack, Wayne Cassidy escaped the asylum days ago, bought a car, and was last seen heading to Ian's Peak."

"I take it to get back at me?"

"I guess that's his plan after what happened in school years ago," Bill replied.

"There's something else," Jack said.

"What?" Bill questioned.

"We got a letter dropped in our mailbox," Jack read aloud. "Your son's here today, gone tomorrow."

"Do you think Wayne was responsible?"

"I'm sure of it now; it's becoming clearer. Wayne mentioned something similar to Mary years ago."

"I'm going to search for the car. The search party is still on."

"Thanks, Bill."

Jack hung up and looked at Anne, confused and worried.

"Well?" Anne asked.

"We think it could be Wayne Cassidy," Jack replied.

"Wayne Cassidy?"

"Yea, do you remember the guy Mary dated back in high school?"

"Why would he do this now after all this time?"

"We think it could be revenge for what we did to him in High School."

Was Wayne Cassidy responsible for abduction, murder, and arson? How could they let him leave the asylum?

Jack's worry has grown. Now there's a motive. They caused Wayne's suffering all those years ago. Mary had nightmares for years and became pregnant with James to escape that traumatic night. She gave up her law degree and become a nurse, so she can take care of her child, a decision she doesn't regret.

"I better warn Mary about Wayne," Anne said.

"That's a good idea," Jack replied.

Chapter Six

I t had been hours since Anne phoned Mary about Wayne. Lost in the memories of an old photo album. Mary sat on a lounge chair, her eyes tracing images of the past. One photo showed a young Mary with a handsome young man, who was popular in primary school with the girls. He didn't start dating Mary until high school. She flipped the photo to reveal his handwritten message: 'To my sugar pie.' Tears rolled down her cheeks. Dressed in her gown, Mary lay on the couch, recalling the night of the dance, an event that terrified her so much she had blocked it out for years.

"Why Wayne? Why are you doing this?"

"Don't worry, sugar pie," he whispered, *"everything will work out for the best."*

"Come on, Wayne, let's play on the swings," she could hear herself when she was younger.

"I love you, my sugar pie," Wayne said.

"I love you too," she replied.

Lost in thought, Mary jumped when the door slammed shut. My arrival back home resulted in her dropping the photo album. While gathering her photographs, one image in particular immediately captivated my attention.

Who could it be?

Mum received a hug from an unidentified person.

"Mum, who is this?" I asked.

"No one," she replied.

"It's him, isn't it?" I inquired, aware of the answer.

"He is the one who kidnapped Paul, isn't he?"

"I don't know what you're talking about."

I was holding the photo firmly, experiencing visions.

"Baby killer," I repeated what I'd heard.

"I don't know what you're talking about," she replied, surprised that I was aware of the past events.

Then, I experienced more of the vision. I still held the photo firmly, and my mum looked at me with concern. She was unsure of what to do. Then, I saw the vision of what happened all those years ago.

Chapter Seven

The vision began with a woman in a hospital bed after giving birth to her baby boy, Gregory Lloyd Cassidy, named after her late father, who died in a car accident the previous year. She also had a thirteen-year-old son, Wayne Cassidy, whom she believed was the devil's son because of his erratic behavior. Despite her warnings, other dismissed her as delusional. Wayne faced bullying in high school but had a girlfriend, Mary Dobson. Since Greg's birth, Wayne often found himself in trouble, even when he did nothing wrong.

"Wayne Cassidy!" his mother would call out to him, "you come here this very instant."

He spent the rest of the day in hiding. Upon his arrival home, his mother would slap him hard enough to leave a red handprint on his face.

"No, Mother," Wayne cried.

"Lies! Always lying!" she yelled.

"No, Mother! I'm telling the truth!"

She grabbed a red-hot frying pan from the stove.

"You know what happens to naughty little sinners? God will punish them!"

"No!" he screamed. "Please, No!"

"Turn around and bend over!" she bellowed at him.

"Please, Mother!"

"I said, turn around now!" she shrieked even louder.

She forced Wayne to turn around. She flung him against a bench, removed his jeans, and then struck his bare backside with a pan, using all her strength. The baby woke up in tears.

"Look what you've done! You've woken the baby!" she said. "You make me sick. Now go to your room, and I don't want to see you for the rest of the night."

Wayne quickly left the room. Threw himself on his bed, and cried louder than the baby, unable to contain himself. Hours went by and Wayne stayed on the bed, straining to hear his mother or the child. All he could hear is the sound of breathing as they both slept.

'If it wasn't for him,' Wayne thought, 'mum wouldn't hit me like she did.'

Slowly, Wayne got up from his bed, his body protesting with aches and pains that were a lingering reminder of the red-hot pan that had struck him. He was in too much pain to put his pants on. He brushed away the tears from his eyes. He couldn't care if he was parading around the house with no clothes on, better still, the streets; maybe the neighbors might see all the marks on the lower part of his body and then realise what sort of beatings he had to put up with. He slowly got up and walked towards the door. Wayne listened closely for any noise, and there wasn't any. He peeped out and saw the room his brat brother was lying in. He slowly opened the door and crept in. His brother, Little Gregory, the devil's son himself, was there. Wayne's going to send his brother back to hell, where he belong.

Wayne looked at him, sleeping peacefully, pretending to be innocent like butter wouldn't melt in his mouth. 'How pathetic,' he thought, disgusted by how the baby was acting. Wayne's heart raced. In a slow, deliberate movement, he kneeled down, picked up a pillow, and with all his might, pressed it against his brother's face.

***

The next day at school, Mary was very sympathetic towards Wayne for losing his brother. They were saying it was cot death that happened to Gregory, which was very common for newborn babies. Wayne looked different. He didn't look like his usual self. He was like another person.

"Are you all right?" Mary finally asked.

"Why shouldn't I be?"

"I don't know. You don't seem to be yourself today."

"How do you want me to act?" Wayne questioned.

"I don't know," she said. "I suppose it's normal after losing your baby brother."

"Losing my baby brother!" Wayne said, laughed out loud. "Losing my baby brother! That's a good one."

"It's not meant to be a joke," she said.

"I'm sorry, I thought it was," he replied. "I'm glad the little brat's dead."

"That's a terrible thing to say," she said, looking more concerned than ever.

"Is it?" he said, laughed even louder. "I killed him with these hands."

"What?"

"You heard me."

40

Mary started getting scared, backing away slowly from him and shaking her head.

"NO!" she screamed out.

"It's true, Mary. I've sent my brother back to hell where he'd belong," Wayne said. "My brother's here today, gone tomorrow."

Wayne slowly walked closer to Mary, who backed away even further.

"Everything's going to be all right," he said.

"Keep away from me!" she screamed.

She ran off, still hearing Wayne laughing wickedly. Mary kept on running. She didn't know what to do about Wayne. She knew Jack's house wasn't far from the park. She had to tell someone. After all, Jack is a close friend, and he might even know what to do.

Mary ran to Jack's house and knocked loudly. Jack answered the door, looking concerned.

"What is it, Mary?" Jack wanted to know.

"It's Wayne. He …." She started but couldn't finish the sentence.

"Mary, what has he done."

"I think he needs help, Jack."

Mary explains to Jack what Wayne had just told her, the look he had given her and the wicked laugh, as if he didn't even care about anything. Jack couldn't believe what he was hearing. He had never liked Wayne much. He always thought Wayne was a strange kid, and the whole family seemed weird. It comes from the parents and the upbringing. It's a good thing young Greg died, or he would have become like the rest of the family.

"Don't worry," Jack said, grinning to himself. "Leave him to me, and I'll decide what to do."

Before too long, every kid in Ian's Peak High School knew about it, and they were talking about Wayne behind his back and laughing at him. They call him "Baby murderer."

They wouldn't dare say it to his face. Mary was upset about what they said about Wayne. She had thought Jack would help him; that's why she'd gone to him. The kids couldn't wait for the night of the school dance. Jack planned something horrible with the entire school, except for Mary, because he knew she wouldn't be part of it.

***

Mum looked at me with profound concern. I clutched Wayne's photo as I experienced a seizure.

"James, what's wrong?" Mary asked.

I couldn't answer her. I couldn't even hear her. My mind was still in the past. I kept seeing the school and the other kids. Some kids I knew as grown-ups. Josh's parents and Sam's dad, Lindsay Peterson, were there. He was the principal even back then. Mum held tight, hoping I would snap out of it soon enough. I had to continue with the past to see what else had happened. I had to know what went on back then to get some answers about what's happening. So, I concentrated once again on learning more about the night that ended up in tragedy, the night that could have started the whole mess of what's happening today, the night of the dance ....

***

The night of the dance came along, and Jack planned to get back at Wayne. Jack Brown, Anne Peters, and Jamie Thompson was there. Jamie

42

married Mary after she became pregnant to forget about this night. They had a baby boy, and christian him James Cedrick Thompson.

The school dance is only one night of the year that all the kids hang around together as one enormous group. Tonight, however, seemed different. There was tension in the air, and they were all dancing to various music.

Tainted Love came on the stereo, and Mary grabbed Wayne by the hand and pulled him up onto the dance floor.

"Come on," she said, "This is my favorite song."

'Don't touch me, please.' The song continued, 'I cannot stand the way you tease.'

Jack went up to his friends in the hall.

"It's time," he said.

One by one, the children left the hall, until only Mary and Wayne remained; they continued dancing. Mr. Peterson just left the hall and didn't notice what was happening around him. As the last notes of the song faded, Mary can see that the room was now completely empty.

"Where is everyone?" she asked curiously.

"How the hell should I know!" Wayne stated.

She looked around and couldn't see anyone. Then Wayne heard noises coming from outside.

"Wayne …. Wayne," the unidentified voice said.

"What's that?" Mary asked.

"Let's have a look," Wayne replied.

Stepping outside into the fresh air. Gazing toward the rear of the school building, Wayne noticed a fire. Moving steadily forward, they pressed on towards the blaze, which burned fiercely with an intense light that illuminated their path. A peculiar sense of wrongness hung in the air, yet both Wayne and Mary found themselves unable to pinpoint the source of their unease or explain the odd feeling. Fueled by dry brush and wind, the fire burned continuously and intensely. As they continued onward, Wayne's sharp eyes caught sight of an object or figure in the distance ahead of their current position. What he saw was a figure, white in appearance, with what looked remarkably like a pair of horns on its head, a sight that startled him. The very devil, a being of pure evil and malice, came back to haunt him, prompting the question of the motivation behind this sinister return.

He gave him the gift that he requested: his baby brother.

"Wayne," the figure spoke.

"What do you want?" Wayne asked.

"You have killed me and sent me down below."

"Gregory?" Wayne questioned.

"Wayne, you have been a bad boy," the figure said, smiling.

"It wasn't my fault. You got to believe me."

"Believe you!" the figure exclaimed.

"You have driven me to it," Wayne said, sounding more pleased with himself.

"If it weren't for you, I would still be in my cot!"

Wayne fell to his knees. Mary realised what was happening. The kids were playing a joke on him, but why?

Why play a terrible prank on someone? What has he ever done to them?

Mary walked backwards slowly because she didn't want to be part of this set-up; it had gone far enough. She looked back to the hall and saw Mr. Peterson watching from the window at the dance. He wasn't doing anything to help Wayne. The other students were teasing him, and all Mr. Peterson could only do was watch, probably having a good chuckle himself. Wayne started hugging his knees tight, sniffling, and crying. The other kids gathered around him and started to laugh and giggle. Mary couldn't believe how mean her friends were.

"Stop it!" she demanded.

Everyone completely ignored her present. Wayne shouldn't be at their school. He was completely insane, a danger to society, and should be kept in a mental institution rather than being allowed to roam freely on the streets. The children continued their relentless taunting of the boy, repeatedly and cruelly chanting the words 'baby killer' to inflict emotional pain.

Wayne looked up and saw the face behind the mask. It was Jack Brown. His mind was on Jack's face, and he would never forget that look as long as he lived. Jack picked up a can of kerosene and poured it in a circle around Wayne, then lit a match that burned furiously around him. He looked scared and desperate.

Ignoring the children who stood in her path, Mary forcefully pushed past them, driven by the pressing need to get to the fire. Wayne suddenly lost control of his temper and went completely berserk, exhibiting wildly erratic behavior. Upon exiting the school, Mr. Peterson retrieved a straitjacket he had discovered in a cupboard within the school doctor's clinic, intending to use it to restrain Wayne until emergency medical services arrived. Wayne's absence lasted a very long time.

***

I escaped the past without panic. Mum remained seated in the living room, observing the sweat streaming down my face.

"Are you okay?" Mum wanted to know.

"I don't know," I replied.

"What happened?"

"I saw what happened at the school dance between Wayne and Josh's dad all those years ago."

"What?"

"I can't explain. The school dance and the joke the others played on Wayne."

"Yes, well, I'm trying to forget. We think he could be the guy who abducted Paul," she said.

"That's the only thing that makes sense," I replied.

I went to go out the front door when Mum stopped me.

"Where are you going?" she wanted to know.

"I need to see Josh and perhaps his dad."

I left to go over to see Josh. Could there be a connection?

That's the only thing that makes sense around here. All the events that happened lately, the school burning down and the murder of Mr. Peterson and the abduction of Paul Brown, one of Jack's children, who was later revealed to be the ringleader of the night of the school dance. Unfortunately, my dad took part in this regrettable matter adds another layer of sadness to the situation.

Chapter Eight

The town folks are still searching for Paul. As day turned to night, the boy remained missing. Officer Butler suspects he is no longer in Ian's Peak. The townspeople searched every house. Despite an exhaustive search of every shed and area of bushland surrounding Ian's Peak, the people of the town still couldn't find him. There were absolutely no clues. The search was becoming increasingly difficult for Anne, and she felt she was nearing her breaking point. The moment she arrived home, a migraine set in, resulting in a painful and intense throbbing headache. The throbbing in her head had continued for hours, feeling as if someone had taken up residence within her skull and was using a sledgehammer to pound against her head. Such intense fear overcame her and all she wanted to do was scream for help. I followed right behind Josh when he left his room. Anne looked pale and tired because she didn't get enough sleep.

"Are you okay, Mum?" Josh asked.

Moments before Anne's arrival, I informed Josh of the vision I had experienced a long time ago at the high school, a vision that depicted his dad as the mastermind behind a scheme involving the rest of Ian's Peak. I recounted the prank pulled on Wayne Cassidy and his dating history with my mum during their school years. They sent Wayne to a mental institution after the night of the dance. Given the circumstances, Josh handled it pretty well, I thought.

"I'll be fine," Anne said. She couldn't even open her eyes to look at us because of the migraine she was having.

"I'm going out to help with the search." Josh said,

"It's almost dark," Anne replied. "They probably will finish soon."

"Don't worry, we won't be long."

"Okay, just be careful."

Josh and I left his mum to rest. They weren't sure what to do next or where to search for Paul.

***

Anne decide to have a bath to ease the pain. The phone rang, but Anne didn't hear it ringing because of the noise of running water and the door being closed. They still have an answering machine that answered the phone.

The machine's message identified the homeowner as Brown's resident. "Leave your number after the beep," said the machine.

"How do you like it?" said the caller. "It's not fun, is it? Having something missing from your life. I've got your boy right with me. Say hello to your mummy!"

"Mum! Help me, please!" Paul pleaded over the phone. "I can't see anything; it's dark. Please come and get me."

The stranger grabbed the phone of Paul.

"So, you thought you got away with it, did you?"

Then he hung up; however, Anne didn't hear her son's pleading for help. Rather than focusing on anything else, she sought refuge in the soothing warmth of the tub, hoping to find relief from the intense headache that had bothered her since the early afternoon hours. With a growing sense of urgency, she desperately hoped for Paul's swift discovery. Although she had fallen into a deep sleep, the same thought persisted in her mind.

***

On the way to help with the search, we picked up Sam, who was waiting anxiously by the side of the road. Josh and Sam were trying to think of unusual places and brainstorming ideas.

In a vision, something came to me. Someone strapped Paul down to an old bench in a dark place. Wayne was also there, lighting a match and blowing it out.

I felt that something was not quite right or perhaps something more was hidden there in the strange and unsettling familiar place. The wall-mounted metal bench, which was equipped with buttons, switches, and levers, appeared oddly familiar, arousing a feeling of déjà vu. It came to James in a flash of insight; he suddenly knew exactly where they could find Paul.

"Cave Death," I said louder than I realised.

"What?" Sam questioned.

"That's where Paul is, Cave Death."

"Of course," Josh replied, "that's one place no one would think to look."

"Okay, we go to my place," I said. "I'll tell Mum I'm staying at your house tonight. We pick up a few things, then head to the cave."

"I'll ring Mum to tell her what's happening. I hope it's not too late." Josh said,

There was another vision, which I didn't let the others know. It was too wild. It was a fire, an evil act of violence, and an explosion in Cave Death, and my mum was involved somehow. I shook off the vision almost as quickly as it came.

***

Anne Brown woke up suddenly; she'd nearly fallen in the water. Her migraine felt slightly less intense. Stepping out of the tub, she grabbed a towel and dried off. In her room, she checked the time, which read 3 am. The last thing she remembered was coming home around 5 p.m. after the search. Josh should be home in bed. To see if Josh was home, Anne went to his bedroom. She first looked at Paul's room. Anne quickly glanced around the room and noticed that nothing was disturbed; the bed was still unmade. She paused at Josh's door, opening it slightly to peek inside. The empty room showed no sign of her son.

Where could he be?

Josh had never been out this late before. Why wasn't he home?

Josh and James may know where Paul is. While hurrying to the lounge room to check if Josh was in the kitchen, the blinking light suddenly diverted Anne's attention on her answering machine. The machine hummed softly as she pressed play, and then Wayne's voice, clear and strong, filled her ears. As she listened to her son's desperate cries for help, she was overcome with emotion and found herself unable to control the tears that streamed down her face. A beep sound signaled the completion of the message. Another message arrived. This time it was Josh.

"Mum," Josh said, "when you get this message, I hope it's not too late. We think we know where Paul could be: Cave Death. We are heading there right now. I've got James and Sam with me."

He concluded the telephone conversation abruptly, offering neither additional dialogue nor a parting message. As the phone rang again, startling Anne, she looked at the machine. Unable to resist for more than a few seconds, she answered the phone, her delay motivated by a cautious hope that the caller was not Wayne once more.

"Hello," she said, quite startled, but she was relieved when it wasn't Wayne's voice but Officer Butler's.

"Anne," Bill said, "I'm just checking to see if James with you?"

"No, and Josh isn't here either."

Anne thoroughly explained the phone call to the officer, detailing the conversations and the timing of them; only after she had completed her report did Bill Butler finally speak.

"I'm coming over to pick you up. We will organise a group to head to Cave Death soon."

Chapter Nine

'Cave Death is just ahead of us,' I thought, but was a little nervous about the idea of entering the cave again after what had happened last time. Because of the Dream Reality powers I developed following Professor Lynx's experiment, I sadly knew in advance what was about to transpire. As we approached the cave, its shadowy, ominous entrance seemed unchanged from the last time we had visited this mysterious place. Unmoving, Josh stood exactly where he had been standing, his eyes intently focused on the cave's dark entrance.

"I didn't think we would ever see this cave again," Josh said.

"That makes two of us." I replied.

"It looks creepy." Sam said with concern.

We went around the cave and prepared for almost anything tonight. Luckily, we thought to bring a few bits and pieces for the journey, including a torch.

'Are we ever going to get out of here alive?' I thought to myself, still remembering the vision I had with Wayne setting the cave on fire and the four of us on the other side of the flames. Mum was there, too. She's going to get there just in time, but I don't know whether anything's going to happen afterwards. I looked around at Josh and Sam. I can't read their minds, but I'm sure they are thinking the same thing I am. We came across a deep-looking hole and looked down into the darkness, but couldn't see anything. Remembering: I recalled throwing the rope down a few years ago, which we are going to do the same thing tonight.

"I'll go first," I announced, easing myself down the long rope.

When I made it to the bottom, I called out to the others. "It's safe to come down."

Sam was the next to climb down, making sure she was careful about doing it. Josh came down last and he slipped and almost fell. He was lucky that he hung on tight and finally made it to where we are. I turned on the torch and shone it around the dark cave once again.

"Nothing has changed," I said.

I had a vague recollection of the path we followed on our last trip here. There was another door; I had no memory of seeing it before. Perhaps it opens into another room, but which one?

That door may hold many answers. I wanted to find out more about the experiment Professor Lynx had left. Entering the room, we discovered an office containing a wooden table, a chair, and an open journal. I examined the journal's contents more closely upon reaching the desk. What I read left me completely speechless. Following closely, Sam noted the mixture of excitement and unease on my face.

"What is it?" she wanted to know.

"It's a journal left by the professor."

"Professor Lynx, the creator of Dream Reality?" Josh questioned.

"That's him," I replied.

"What does it say?" Josh wanted to know.

I read, "Professor Lynx, 1892," then continued, "The Dark Secret of Ian's Peak: I have discovered the world's most powerful experiment, 'Dream Reality'. Whoever enters this experiment will see things that have already happened, happening, or are yet to happen in a vision or a dream. I had a dream of a young boy who will enter the world of Dream Reality and see wonderful things and bad things. Use the power wisely and beware. They might have found me and want to kill me for my ability to foresee the future."

"I wondered what had happened to him?" Sam asked.

"I'm not sure," I said. I looked through the journal from the beginning of the book. I found something of some interest about the project called Dream Reality and when he first started this experiment. He had claimed God had contacted him to build this machine, so someone out there could have this power of Dream Reality. He wanted someone to stop crimes from happening.

'I must be that someone.' I thought to myself.

I continued looking through the journal and came across descriptions that we've known as a TV set, video recorder, and even a microwave oven.

"Look at these," I said to the others. Josh had a good look at the sketches but couldn't believe his eyes. Not even in your wildest imagination back in 1892 could ever think of descriptions like these.

"That is so incredible." Sam said.

"He must have seen people watching TV in his dreams," I said, "and the next morning sketched it on a piece of paper."

I also came across a picture of someone hanging from a tree. The professor had seen a hanging in a dream, and right underneath the sketch it read: 'Professor's hanging tree.'

"He must have seen his own hanging." Josh said.

"I think you're right there, and probably was waiting for that day to happen." I replied.

"That must have been awful." Sam said.

"According to Professor Lynx, after admitting there is Dream Reality, he can see moving pictures on a box and a big plane in the air called a jumbo jet. The folks in Ian's Peak thinks I'm crazy and an evil old man. They are going to hang me."

"That's enough!" Sam demands. "I don't want to hear anymore."

Given my premonition of the explosion and the cave's collapse within the next two hours, we better get out of here quick. I also have the desire to ensure the journal's safety. I opened my backpack, which provided ample room for the safekeeping of the journal.

Something distracted Josh that he turned around in all directions.

"What's that?" he questioned.

"What?" I asked.

The sound came again, sounding like some shuffling noise and groaning coming from another room somewhere in the dark cave. It couldn't be far from where we are.

"That!" Josh said.

We quickly left the room. Taking the lead, I walked ahead of the others to guide them on our journey. The sound seemed to get closer and closer. We finally came across the room where the sound was coming from. Upon entering, the room was so dark it was nearly impossible to see. With our torch held high, we carefully searched the room upon entry, our beams eventually finding movement in the far corner, showing something is there. Drawing closer, it became apparent to us that the individual in question was, in fact, Paul himself.

"Paul!" Josh screamed out.

Wayne strapped Paul down to the bench, just as I had been strapped down a few years ago, where the Dream Reality experiment originated. He was still wearing the same clothes that he was last seen in on the day he'd disappeared. Josh found Paul gagged and blindfolded. When we got closer to him, Paul freaked out. He didn't know who was there because he thought Wayne had come back.

"Paul, it's me," Josh said. Paul recognised his brother's voice. We removed the gag and then unstrapped him and got him to his feet.

"Josh, where's Mum?" Paul asked. He was so glad to see his brother again that he threw his arms around him to give him a big hug. For the first time in Josh's life, he didn't push him away and hugged him right back.

"It's all right, Paul. I'm here and so are James and Sam."

Suddenly, another vision came to me. It was terrible and frightening. A fire was starting with the four of them stuck on the wrong side of the flames, not knowing how to get out. Wayne was on the other side laughing and said, "Burn, burn, burn!"

"Quick, we got to leave, now!" I said, "there's going to be a terrible fire."

"Did you see something?" Sam wanted to know.

"Yeah," I said, "quick, we better hurry."

The air was thick with the smell of kerosene, a heavy, oily scent that filled my lungs. Turning around, I came face to face with Wayne Cassidy, his long hair and a broad-shouldered frame that filled the doorway, a solid 150 pounds, barring our only way out. His bell bottoms and platform shoes screamed 1970s fashion. He had coal-black hands covered in grime and a dirt-smudged face. With a determined grip, he held the match, ready to ignite it against the rough stone. Doing so could explode the cave.

"Don't do it, Wayne!" he heard a voice from behind him. Wayne turned around startled and recognised the person who spoke, someone he liked all those years ago.

"Sugar Pie," he said.

"Wayne, put the match down. You don't want to harm them." Mary. pleaded.

"No!"

Another voice startled Wayne even more. The voice belonged to his enemy. It was the voice of Josh and Paul's father; it was the voice of Jack Brown.

"Put the match down!" Jack said. "It's me you want, not the kids."

"Mary," Wayne said, "get him away from me." He went to light the match when Mary distracted him again.

"Wayne, don't light the match yet. Jack is just leaving." She said, looking directly at Jack, who would not budge.

"I hope you know what you're doing," Jack whispered to Mary. She nodded slowly so Wayne couldn't catch on what they were planning to do. Jack left the cave quietly, so did Officer Butler and the others. Mary found herself alone with Wayne and the children.

"Wayne, just let these kids go," Mary pleaded with him.

"But, Sugar Pie, this is a game," Wayne said.

"What game?" Mary wanted to know.

"The three little pigs and I'm the big bad wolf."

"But there are four of them."

"I see what you are trying to do. You think I'm a fruitcake, don't you?"

"No, Wayne," she said. Wayne walked over to the other side of the cave mumbling to himself, "they say I'm evil. Do you think I don't know what they are saying?" He then said, "No, Mary, I'm not the evil one, it's you and them."

Mary signaled to the kids to leave the cave. Josh took Paul out first, with Sam following slowly behind. After that, I started to leave and then I turned to mum with concern.

"Will you be, okay?" I whispered, which Wayne overheard. He turned around and could see the kids were nowhere in sight except for me, and I also walked out of the cave as fast as I could.

"You shouldn't have done that!" Wayne said, raising his voice.

"They are only kids," Mary replied.

"You're like the others, always against me."

"No, of course I'm not. I love you, Wayne," Mary said. "it doesn't have to be this way."

"Yes, it does," he said, picking up the kerosene can.

 "I've always loved you, sugar pie."

He poured kerosene all over his body, holding a box of matches. Mary strolled backwards. She knew he was crazy; she could see it in his eyes that he was going to light the match, and she didn't want to be in the firing line.

"Wayne, don't please," she pleaded.

"Ashes to Ashes!" he said, then struck the match at the side of the box and lit it as if he was lighting a candle on a birthday cake. Wayne's shocking chapter of his past had finally come to a close, bringing with it a sense of relief and closure.

Epilogue

I t's been a few weeks since the incident at Cave Death with Wayne and Mum. Now that the long, hot summer break has ended, we are back at school and ready to begin classes again. After the devastating fire, the school is still under reconstruction and will reopen at a later date. We had to take the bus to the next town for classes because our school is undergoing necessary repairs, and this will continue until the repairs have finished. Wayne's actions resulted in a self-inflicted explosion, causing his mum in shock, leading to her being in hospital, although she's expected to be discharged soon.

'She was very lucky,' I thought to myself.

I recall the incident. I remember the cave's complete destruction by the explosion. A figure pushed mum out of the cave. The five-foot figure had no shirt. He was unshaven, his pants torn, and his beard long. Rising, he looked at me. This figure seemed to be from another time. I've seen him before in my other dreams. Professor Lynx had come there that day to rescue my mum. He must have seen what was going to happen or he must have heard me screaming for help and came from another time to help me out on this one. He knew Wayne was just too strong for me to handle.

I'm glad life is returning to normal. We recently held a funeral service for Sam's dad, Lindsay Peterson, just a short time ago. Every single person in town came to pay their final respects to the principal, a testament to his profound impact on the community. Although Sam continues to have the support of her mum, the absence of her dad creates a significant void in her life, a loss that I deeply empathise with and understand completely from her perspective. I am surprised to see that Josh and Paul are much closer now; I never thought that would ever happen. It's my belief that Josh will keep a close watch over Paul for the rest of their lives, or at least until Paul's old enough to look after himself. Something like a kidnapping, usually strength family ties, forcing members to rely on each other for emotional and practical support during a time of crisis. Only when something is lost, that we realise its value. even briefly. Josh's situation perfectly illustrates this point, highlighting how we often take things for granted until they're gone. With a bit of luck, something like this won't ever happen in Ian's Peak again. I'm still battling with keeping everyone together.

Mum being in hospital, I'm learning to defend and look after myself. I'm learning more and more about the Dream Reality experiment. Even though it's the end of Cave Death, it won't be the end of the powers I have gained from the experiment. The only ones that know about the power is Josh, Sam, and of course myself. We be using it to help people. I was sitting on the bus on the way home from school, which was after 3 p.m., when something came to me in a vision, lasted only a few minutes, something strange, something that I have never seen before in Ian's Peak.

***

A Man in his late forties was sitting on the edge of a bed visiting an elderly lady. It looked like it could be a hospital. This man has no name or, at this stage, even a face, but all you can see is his moustache.

Where is this place?

Could it be Ian's Peak hospital? Only in time we can tell.

He was wearing a business suit and was carrying a briefcase, which showed that he worked somewhere in Ian's Peak and has his own business, but it's hard to tell what business he was in. He said goodbye to the elderly woman in bed and gave her a kiss on the cheek before exiting out the door and down the corridor. There didn't seem to be anyone around, except for a cleaner polishing the floors, who looked very busy and concerned about what he was doing. He went up to the elevators, and there were three of them in a row. He pressed the button to go down. The floor number on the side of the elevator read 6, which showed that he was on the sixth floor, and he wanted to get down to maybe the first floor. He looked around while waiting for the elevator to arrive. The door of the elevator opened pretty quickly. He entered, which left him in the small box on his own. Since it was a little past 7 pm, he headed out, wanting to avoid being late and ensure he had a sufficient amount of rest for his early morning schedule. This unknown person noticed he hadn't pressed the button yet.

'That's funny,' he thought to himself, 'I'm sure I pressed the button.'

So, he pressed it again and waited, and before his eyes, he noticed that the light of the button went off again.

'What's going on here?' he thought to himself.

Pressing it again made all the buttons turn on and off and went berserk. He had never, ever seen that happen in all the time he had visited the hospital. He felt as if the elevator was going down faster than the normal speed.

'What's going on?' he asked himself again.

He couldn't bear the speed that the elevator was going at, so he fell to the ground and huddled in the corner. His heart was racing at a hundred miles an hour. He curled up like a ball, waiting to see what was going to happen next. He thought that someone had messed around with the elevator and cut it so it would fall.

Suddenly, with no warning whatsoever, the elevator crashed to the bottom with a big thud. For a few minutes, he thought he was unconscious and then he became conscious again without realising where he was or what had happened. The door of the elevator opened much quicker than it had closed. There was something that made little sense at all. It looked cloudy outside, like there wasn't an outside. He got to the edge of the elevator to see what was going on and who or what was out there. He couldn't believe it. His mouth opened wider than anyone could imagine, and he was ready to scream the most terrifying scream anyone could scream, so his mouth opened and out came …

The Dream Continues…..

Part Two:
The Basement

Prologue

A Man in his late forties was sitting on the edge of a bed visiting an elderly lady. It looked like it could be a hospital. This man has no name or, at this stage, even a face, but all you can see is his moustache.

Where is this place?

Could it be Ian's Peak hospital? Only in time we can tell.

He was wearing a business suit and was carrying a briefcase, which showed that he worked somewhere in Ian's Peak and has his own business, but it's hard to tell what business he was in. He said goodbye to the elderly woman in bed and gave her a kiss on the cheek before exiting out the door and down the corridor. There didn't seem to be anyone around, except for a cleaner polishing the floors, who looked very busy and concerned about what he was doing. He went up to the elevators, and there were three of them in a row. He pressed the button to go down. The floor number on the side of the elevator read 6, which showed that he was on the sixth floor, and he wanted to get down to maybe the first floor. He looked around while waiting for the elevator to arrive. The door of the elevator opened pretty quickly. He entered, which left him in the small box on his own. Since it was a little past 7 pm, he headed out, wanting to avoid being late and ensure he had a sufficient amount of rest for his early morning schedule. This unknown person noticed he hadn't pressed the button yet.

'That's funny,' he thought to himself, 'I'm sure I pressed the button.'

So, he pressed it again and waited, and before his eyes, he noticed that the light of the button went off again.

'What's going on here?' he thought to himself.

Pressing it again made all the buttons turn on and off and went berserk. He had never, ever seen that happen in all the time he had visited the hospital. He felt as if the elevator was going down faster than the normal speed.

'What's going on?' he asked himself again.

He couldn't bear the speed that the elevator was going at, so he fell to the ground and huddled in the corner. His heart was racing at a hundred miles an hour. He curled up like a ball, waiting to see what was going to happen next. He thought that someone had messed around with the elevator and cut it so it would fall.

Suddenly, with no warning whatsoever, the elevator crashed to the bottom with a big thud. For a few minutes, he thought he was unconscious and then he became conscious again without realising where he was or what had happened. The door of the elevator opened much quicker than it had closed. There was something that made little sense at all. It looked cloudy outside, like there wasn't an outside. He got to the edge of the elevator to see what was going on and who or what was out there. He couldn't believe it. His mouth opened wider than anyone could imagine, and he was ready to scream the most terrifying scream anyone could scream, so his mouth opened and out came.

AAAAAAHHHHHH.

The faceless man collapsed in the elevator right before this unknown creature; he saw a horrible being, a being that should and belongs in hell.

Chapter One

1860–30 years before the experiment

The night felt unbearably hot as the heat wave moved from north to south. In the history books, the story of how this town of Ian's Peak came to be what it is today left out minor details of what happened during the town's formative years. It was only a year or two after the settlers arrived in town that they constructed a hospital, which they named Ian's Peak Hospital. They had moved from up north; the settlers believed that the heat wave was following them; the new future town folks were in the wagon, and some men had become sick from an unknown illness. Nobody knew where the sickness was coming from or the cause of the dreadful disease; all they knew was they would have to set up camp soon, or they might start losing their loved ones. The wagon stopped suddenly, and the folks tired from not sleeping were wondering what was happening.

They could hear footsteps around the side of the wagon. Sounds like bags and boxes were being moved around, but most of the folks fell back asleep except for just a few, who got out and helped; one volunteer was Dr. Ian Peak. The district had never seen a doctor as well as he was. He was solidly built and knew more about medicine than any other doctor alive; he was also concerned about people in the group getting sick suddenly; his assistant, Nurse Yvonne, wasn't as caring as the Doctor. Yvonne was a vicious woman who thought of no one else but herself. She was helping to set up camp that night alongside the Doctor. Each day, they seemed to have more sick men, who appeared to have the same symptoms as those who were ill or dying.

'That's strange,' one woman thought, 'It's a sickness that's not affecting any women or children in the camp, only men.'

To her friends, the woman, Kody, was about 29 years old, and her husband, James Thompson, the first Thompson ever to set foot in Ian's Peak, looked ill himself. The couple had a bright-eyed five-year-old son, Jonathan, who is getting into things, always asking, 'Why have we stopped?' 'Why are people sick?' 'Where are we?'

His parents couldn't answer any of these questions; how could they answer such questions when they don't know themselves? Kody waited patiently to see what would happen next; her husband and son were fast asleep next to her,

'Lucky them.' She'd thought to herself.

Kody was annoyed because she had been awake for days. Nurse Yvonne went to the back of the wagon, opened the flap where Kody was sitting up and looked straight at the strange Nurse.

"It's time to get out; it's all set up and ready for everyone," Yvonne said, looking somewhat pleased with herself; she just looked straight through Kody as if she'd never existed.

"Where are we?" Kody demanded.

"You will know soon enough," Yvonne said, "like everyone else."

Kody didn't argue with the woman or liked her very much. She woke her husband and son and got out of the wagon to help with the rest of the setup, along with hundreds of other men, women, and children.

Kody asked no more questions; it wasn't her place to ask anything. If she wanted to know something, it would have to come from her husband, James; he also thought he wasn't worthy of asking such questions. James might be the man of the house; he was also a simple man who didn't believe in argument or conflict over anything. The couple took the boxes out of the wagon like the rest of the group and set up a tent; quite a few sick people were in the group. They looked as if they were dying. James was usually a healthy young man, but he started showing symptoms like the others. Kody and their son Jonathan were in shock over James' sudden illness. He had to be in quarantine as well, and no one could visit them in the tent because they, too, might have caught this unexplained illness if they hadn't already. The wives and children can still see their loved ones through the tent, where they are resting to fight this illness.

"Mama," said Jonathan, in his small childish voice, "what's wrong with Papa?"

"He's not feeling well, Jonathan," Kody could only say; that's because she didn't know what was happening to any of these people, let alone her husband.

She doesn't understand any of this; how can she expect her five-year-old son to understand? Jonathan could remember all the good things about Papa, primarily when they used to fly kites and play the ball out in the open ground at their last home. Now, he could see how weak his Papa had become compared to a week ago.

Yvonne has a town meeting, and they all gather around this woman who claims to be in charge.

"I'm sorry to inform you," Yvonne said, not having a care in the world, "but we have lost two men overnight. We had to bury them in unmarked graves."

"What is going on?" demanded one wife.

"Surely you and Dr Peak know by now what is happening," another distressed wife called out.

"We are doing everything we can," Yvonne replied with a sneaky grin.

"That's not good enough!" Kody called out.

"Who said that?" Yvonne demanded calmly.

"I did, Kody Thompson," Kody replied as she showed herself. Yvonne looked through her as if she was responsible for this whole mess.

"My husband, James, has the same symptoms. Is he too going to die like the others," she demanded.

"I don't know; perhaps we'll all going to die," Yvonne replied sarcastically.

"How come this unexplained disease only affects the men in the camp and not any of the women or children?" Kody wanted to know.

"I don't know the answer to that." Yvonne insists, "The meeting is over."

Yvonne left the group with little explanation or even an apology for what was happening to their husbands. Kody noticed Yvonne looked as if she was pregnant, but that's impossible; she's not married or even had a man in her life, not that anyone would ever sleep with her.

Another night had gone by, and there was another death, and yet again, Yvonne buried the body in another unmarked grave, waking no one. Something terrible is happening in this camp, but no one knows what.

Dr Ian Peak was getting concerned because Yvonne had never woken him when there was a death; he's got no choice but to take her word for it. However, he feels responsible for the townsfolk, because they are in his care and rely on his experience as a doctor, and somehow feels as if he has failed them. He was getting a little suspicious about what was happening and something weird about the strange-looking Nurse. He'd thought that there's something far worse was happening at the campsite than meeting the eye. Ever since Yvonne joined the nursing team, Dr Peak had reservations that something wasn't quite right; he doesn't even know how she even got a nursing position because he usually has the final say. She just turned up as a nurse, with no approval of being one. There is something about this woman. People don't just automatically get sick and die within a day after getting ill.

The doctor, a man of great skill and intellect, is determined to find out what is going on, and he will not rest until he has succeeded. Jenkins Lynx, who also sensed something strange in the air, was alongside the Doctor when he observed the Doctor's poor health, causing him to contemplate the possibility of contracting the same illness plaguing everyone else. Since their youth, Jenkins had been not only Dr. Ian Peak's partner but also his dearest friend, a testament to their enduring bond and a man of unwavering integrity, one of the truly good guys. Jenkins always supported the Doctor. Despite a general lack of understanding regarding their relationship, it was evident that they had maintained an unbreakable bond since the beginning of their friendship. No matter what the reason, it is quite clear that deactivating the Doctor in such an abrupt fashion was wholly unacceptable under any circumstances. Jenkin, instead of pressuring him, patiently allowed him to reveal the information at his own pace and in his own way.

Chapter Two

"James Thompson," Sam stated, examining my school assignment, "this wouldn't be acceptable as a history report."

"Give me one good reason, why not?" I curiously asked, knowing that Sam could be right.

"Everyone knows what happened in the History of Ian's Peak."

"Yeah, but what if the history books were wrong?" I said, needing some clarification.

"They are never wrong," Sam said, looking at me strangely.

"How do you know," I said, "were you there?"

"No, of course, I wasn't there." Sam replied.

"Well, I have seen what happened," I said, "last night in my dream."

"You dreamed all this?" Sam asked, even though she knew the answer.

"Yes, all I've written, but I'm sure there's more. I will hand it in once I get the full story and the proof."

"Who would believe you, though?" Sam said.

"I know!"

"What are you going to tell them?" Sam questioned, sounding more sympathetic than angry, "This is all true because I had a dream last night of something that happened over a hundred years ago, and by the way, I have dream reality powers."

"I guess not." I said, "Never thought about it."

Sam knew I was upset that she didn't support me. She might be right. I might end up in a mental health facility.

"There's something else, isn't there, James?" Sam finally asked after a few minutes of silence.

"I had a dream the other night that someone visited his mum at Ian's Peak Hospital, and when he entered the elevator, he disappeared without a trace."

"Do you know what happened to him?"

"When the elevator door opened, I can see that he was taken to a darkened place somewhere. I think it's inside our hospital; this unknown man screamed, and that's when I woke up." James explained.

"Do you think something strange is happening at the hospital?" Sam questioned.

"All I know is something strange is happening," I replied. "I know that whatever I dreamed about that happened over a hundred years ago has something to do with what could be happening now."

"That's huge," Sam said. "What are you going to do?"

"There's only one thing I can do," I replied. "We must work out what all this means and try to stop it. I received this power for a reason."

"Have you got any ideas so far?" Sam asked.

"I've got something," I said. "A review of decades of archived newspaper articles indicated a recurring series of strange occurrences within the specific elevator."

"What kinds of things?" Sam curiously inquired.

I provided Sam with an online article. My mum and I worked at that hospital. The elevator I clean was in my dream.

Sam checked each clipping on the missing men.

"It seem to be only men that went missing, not a single woman or child had disappeared," Sam said.

"Yes, I figured that out too," I replied, my voice low and thoughtful. "Hold on, there's something else I need to mention!" A shiver of unease running down my spine.

"What?" she questioned, her voice betraying her confusion. Sam's bright, curious eyes fixed on me, her gaze intense as she eagerly pressed for details about my discovery and thoughts.

"Have a look at the date of each disappearance; notice the strange pattern." I mentioned.

"These events all occurred on November 18th, a date that repeats every ten years." Sam said,

"Have you noticed the name of all that vanished?" I questioned,

"They shared the same name," Sam remarked. "They must be related."

"But just look at the name!" Unable to contain my excitement and desperate to hear what she had to say, I immediately interrupted with my own words, unable to bear waiting a moment longer.

"Each missing person's name is Peak."

"Peak, you mean like the town Ian's Peak?" Sam curiously asked,

"Exactly, they are all related to Dr Ian Peak, the town's founder and in my dreams, I had from 1860," I said.

"I wonder if he's related to Zac Peak?"

"I think the last guy that disappeared ten years ago was his dad," I replied. "Look at the article about the last guy who disappeared."

"Mr Peak was last seen entering Ian's Peak Hospital, where he said goodbye to his wife, Marilyn, and his four-year-old son, Zachary Peak." Sam reads.

"Wow," Sam remarked, "This looks like revenge on the Doctor."

"Yeah, it sounds like it!" I replied.

"In a couple of days, it will be the eighteenth and the 10th anniversary since the last disappearance; if my calculations are correct, the guy I have seen in my dream should be disappearing on that day."

"Do you know the time?" Sam asked,

"Yeah," I said. "According to the article, each disappearance happened around 7:06 p.m."

"That's a strange time – 7:06." Sam stated.

"That's what I thought until I work out what it means,"

"What's that?" Sam questioned.

"Breaking it into parts, you have 6 hours, followed by 60 minutes in an hour, and then 6 minutes. The Devil's number 666."

"So, what's the plan?" Sam asked.

"I will call Josh and let him know what's happening, and then we all meet at the hospital to decide what to do next."

"James, be careful; this sounds dangerous." Sam stated.

"I know, right!" I said.

Chapter Three

During my standard hospital shift, the beeping of machines formed a dull background to my growing unease; I predicted that someone would go missing from this elevator in a couple of days. The newspaper clippings detailed the event was scheduled to begin at precisely 7:06. I'm going to be on the lookout for anything that seems out of the ordinary, paying close attention to any unusual behavior that might occur. Knowing Sam and Josh's history of being such great helpers, I have full confidence that they will be present to lend a hand on that day. I didn't tell Sam that Nurse Yvonne was an uncanny resemblance to the nurse from my vision of the 19th century; it was a secret I kept from her. I don't think she'd cope well with it. This situation is proving extremely difficult for me to manage, making it unrealistic to expect others to handle it more easily. My inspection of the elevator found its operation and design to be without fault or unusual characteristics. Although this looks like a normal elevator, it's anything but ordinary. To help with the inspection, Josh was there alongside me. I still remember the look on his face when I first told him the whole story; being friends all our lives, I should know what he was thinking. It wasn't until late yesterday that I finally told him, but given the difficult circumstances, he took it on the chin.

"James," I remember him saying, "that is extreme shit."

"I know Josh," I remember saying to him, "it's more extreme than Crazy Wayne when we entered Cave Death earlier this year."

Against my expectations, Josh had Zac with him. Josh, unable to maintain secrecy any longer, declared that the truth about Zac's dad's fate, a mystery of the last ten years, would soon come to light. Like many others, I suspect he seeks answers and resolution to his inquiries. Sam's also lending a hand.

I now know who Mr. Peak will visit in a couple of days. His mum, Elaine Peak, is in room C24. Elaine is also Zac's grandmother. She had a stroke five years ago, impaired her speech. I chatted with her earlier today while cleaning.

"James," Josh called out from the elevator shaft, "there is something down here."

"What did you find?" I curiously asked.

"I don't know if it means anything. This is unbelievable!"

"That's weird," Zac said,

I joined Josh and Zac in the elevator. They were looking at something strange. Someone had sketched a multi-headed beast, from our childhood Sunday school stories, in the elevator.

"That looks familiar," I said. "I've seen the image before, but not from church."

"Where?" Josh curiously asked.

I retrieved Professor Lynx's journal from my backpack and turned to a specific page. The Professor had also drawn the same picture. Underneath, he wrote -The Prince of Darkness: Lucifer.

"Lucifer?" Josh questioned.

"You remember, Lucifer is another name for the devil. We are dealing with the beast."

"Look at this, Josh," I said, handing him the journal.

Upon receiving the journal, Josh gazed up at me in wonder.

"How's that possible?" Pointing to the very last entry on the journal's last page, Josh declared, "My last examination of this journal concluded with this entry, indicating that there was nothing more added to it after that time. It seems to me, other entries has been added to the journal"

"What!" Zac said, "I don't get it; how would that be possible?"

I just stared at Zac, figuring out how to explain everything to him.

"It's hard to explain, Zac; all I could tell you, is that this Professor Lynx from 1890 is communicating to me through this journal."

"Really," Zac said, "That's incredible."

"James, watch out for the nurse," Josh reads. "I am rapidly coming up with a plan. In the basement there's a wormhole, this portal is like a connection, a bridge between the distant point in time representing the past and the future, creating a pathway across time. With the destruction of the basement in 1860, all the events happen after that, including all of the subsequent disappearances will be erased from existence, thereby guaranteeing the safety and well-being of all involved. But you'll possess a unique and personal recollection of the experience that only you will retain. Your friends will not remember the event; their minds will be completely blank regarding this incident."

Josh stared at the page for a few minutes before Realising it was more dangerous than he initially thought.

"So…" Josh finally said, "None of us will remember this afterwards, only you?"

"Apparently," I replied.

Josh persisted in his reading, noting that the destruction of the portal would rewrite the future, preventing all the current negative happenings and paving the way for a much brighter and improved future.

"So …." Zac said, sounding speechless, "When all this is over, does that mean my dad won't disappear either?"

"I'm confident he won't vanish, and your grandmother may not have suffered that stroke years ago." I stated,

"That would be so cool; I miss my grandmother, the way she was."

The unsolved mystery of the disappearances still haunted those who know the story from the elevator every ten years.

What's going to happen to Zac's uncle? Should we be late? I predicted he would disappear in two days.

Why are Ian's Peak residents misleading us about what really happened in the history? Maybe they believed the historical lies.

Uncovering this town and hospital secrets. Stuart Peak disappears in a couple of days; time's running out. We must investigate this urgently because of the grim situation and the impending danger of someone being lost to the underworld.

Chapter Four

In the settlement, a chilling trend developed as the men vanished one after the other, creating an atmosphere of suspicion, fear, and unanswered questions. For a second time, Nurse Yvonne made the painful announcement about the necessity of burying the bodies in unmarked graves, a task that filled her with sorrow. Jenkins and Dr. Peak felt increasingly suspicious of the strange nurse, overwhelmed by curiosity and a growing belief that she was behind the recent events.

In Dr. Ian Peak's mind, there was no doubt that Yvonne was responsible for the unexplained sickness that had befallen the town and caused the townspeople's deaths. The Doctor has found out the mysterious happenings in this developing town through his observations of Nurse Yvonne's morning routine. Everyone knows that a good night's sleep is essential for proper daytime functioning, yet the nurse appeared exhausted, suggesting she had been working all night and not sleeping at all during the day. To discover Yvonne's true character, Dr. Ian Peak, on one particular night, engaged in a clandestine act of deception: he pretended to sleep the entire night while actually remaining awake, carefully observing Yvonne's activities while the other friendly, devoted people were asleep. It would have been around three in the morning when Ian Peak heard a disturbance coming from the isolation tent.

The Doctor had to investigate what was happening out there. He'd noticed that someone in a cape was looking suspicious in the distance. Ian Peak was trying to be silent through the bushes, heading towards the tent and hiding behind the tree.

He was watching her every move from a great distance, careful not to go too close for Yvonne to notice.

When this unknown person left the tent carrying something that looked like a body wrapped up in a blanket, Ian Peak knew who this person was leaving the tent. He wasn't sure until she'd turned around. The light glimpse on her face was when he'd instantly recognised her; it was the nasty-looking Nurse Yvonne.

'What is she doing?' Ian thought, 'And what is she doing carrying around this unknown body in a blanket?'

The Doctor knew damn well that he couldn't answer his questions, but he also knew he didn't need to be a genius to figure out what was wrapped up in the blanket. Yvonne hadn't noticed Ian was behind her. She continued to carry on what she was doing and concentrated on where she was going. Ian slowly and quietly followed her to where she was taking this unknown body. He stepped on a pile of rocks that was loose on the ground, which made a noise. Not too loud, though, but it was loud enough to disturb Yvonne from doing what she was doing for just a split second. She turned around and investigated the darkness, but nobody was there, so she continued her journey. Ian Peak wasn't that far behind her, but far enough that she couldn't see him because darkness swallowed him up.

'What is she doing?' he repeated the same unanswered question.

When Ian Peak got close enough to the Nurse, she had her hands in the air for just a split second with the body rising above the nurse's head without touching it, and then the body dropped into the deep hole she had dug in the ground earlier that day. Whatever he had witnessed was the strangest thing he had ever seen; a light was coming from the hole and lifted the body into the air higher than the tallest mountain in the world. Yvonne was standing there, raising her hand as if she was showing someone the direction of what was up. Dr. Ian Peak couldn't believe what he had just witnessed; coming from the hole was some kind of beast head, larger than life. The beast's eyes were glowing as red as fire, flames shooting out, capturing the empty shell of its body thousands of meters in the air. Ian was rubbing his eyes, not believing any of this. Was he dreaming? Hoping that somehow someone would wake him up from this nightmare. He knew no one would wake him up, or that this wasn't a dream; what he'd just witnessed had just happened, and he hoped he wouldn't see anything like this again.

'What can he do?' he asked himself. 'I know that no one is going to believe me if I told anyone.'

Chapter Five

Upon waking, a sharp headache assaulted my senses; it directly resulted from the intense and unforgettable dream that had captivated my mind throughout the night. I looked up towards the desk; the clock read 8:30 a.m. I have to start work at nine. Leaping from my bed, I ran down the hall to take a shower.

***

As tomorrow marks the 18th of November, I expect a disappearance; someone will vanish from this elevator, pulled into a mysterious, unseen world concealed within the hospital building itself. I had to be constantly alert, looking for and expecting any signs of something out of the ordinary or any unusual activity that was about to happen. Hopefully, I'd get to the elevator first, sparing another person from that basement creature. One thing became clear to me: the creature in my dream and the picture Josh found in the elevator depicted the devil. The only thing I didn't quite understand was why Nurse Yvonne had been so angry with all these people all those years ago and why she'd been sacrificing humans to the beast.

It could have something to do with the Nurse being pregnant. Did her baby have a father? Or was the Devil the father? That part of this craziness frightens me the most because of the unknown. I'm sure I will figure out everything soon enough and work out this mystery of what happened over a century ago and the problem that we are facing today.

I know that if we don't find out the answer and stop this man from disappearing or even eliminate the whole mess Yvonne had brought to the hospital, it will continue with this date every ten years. So, I knew this needed to end tomorrow, or there could be severe consequences.

"James," Sam hollered to me from afar, "I didn't think we would make it."

Sam, Josh and even Zac were trying to get my attention. Still, I was miles away just thinking about Zac's uncle, who we need to save from this beast. Hopefully, somehow, destroy the basement without destroying the hospital; after all, it was the basement that started this whole mess. I wish Professor Lynx could help; he gives me the dream reality powers. The Professor is trying to tell me something, but what? I learned that this happened many years before the dream reality powers and even before the Professor was born; however, I felt he has some connection somehow, but what? I remember in my dream just the other night that a Lynx was helping Dr. Ian Peak, who was following Nurse Yvonne. Could it be possible that Lynx, in my dream, was a relative of the good old professor? Maybe the Professor's dad!

Eventually, I'm sure I will receive answers to all my questions. None of this situation makes any sense to me at this moment. The town's past includes the unearthing of the city Ian Peak by the townsfolk. It was thirty years later when Professor Lynx's uncovering of the Dream Reality experiment resulted in his gaining of this amazing power. At the time of his death, the professor had not yet reached the age of thirty. I read that when Professor Lynx was 28; he destroyed Cave Death and everything within the dark cave.

"Is everything alright?" Josh was curious.

"Huh?" I uttered.

"What's happening?" Sam asked curiously, but with a tone that suggested she may not want to hear the answer.

"I'm just thinking," I could only say.

"About what?" Josh curiously asked.

"Just the dream I had last night," I said, "Trying to put the puzzle together about what happened all those years ago. Hoping that it would give me some clue so I can stop this mess from happening."

"It must have been pretty bad,' Sam said, 'you look quite distant."

"All set for this adventure?" I inquired.

"I hope so," Josh said. "Zac was helping me. I hope you know what you're doing?"

"Of course I do," I said. "Just put it this way: We haven't got much of a choice, have we?"

"I guess not." With a nervous grin, Josh said, "Let's get to work."

"We only have one chance to get this right," I said, attempting to sound convincing. "So let's do it right and even triple-check everything."

Chapter Six

'I suppose this is it, there is no turning back now,' I thought to myself, attempting to stay calm and hide my true feelings of being nervous, struggling against the overwhelming anxiety.

The extreme risks involved are making me reconsider this mission. I'm not the only one feeling nervous about facing the uncertainties ahead; my friends, especially Josh, since he's coming along, share my apprehension as we prepare to enter this uncharted territory tomorrow night.

"Are you sure we're ready?" Josh curiously asked, sounding as excited as the first time we entered the cave years ago. He knew that this mission would be far worse than the last one.

"No," I could only say, "but we just have to be."

"Have you guys got everything?" Sam asked.

"Yeah, rope and torch are the main things we'll need," Josh replied with anxiety.

"We still have a little over 24 hours before we go down to the basement, and we need to wait for Stuart to press the button and waiting for the elevator." I said.

"James Thompson to the nurse station." said the voice over the intercom.

"That's me," I said as I wandered towards the elevator. "It sounds like Nurse Yvonne."

"I thought you said she's got the day off?" Sam reminded me.

"She supposed to have." I replied.

"Do you think that she might know something?" Sam asked.

"I'm not sure!" I said, continued, "There is something I haven't told either of you."

"What?" Josh asked curiously, and by the looks of Sam, she was very curious to know what I was about to tell them.

"Nurse Yvonne …. Well, she was the same nurse that appeared in my dream over a hundred years ago." I said, thinking that I probably sounded crazy.

"Are you sure?" Sam asked, not sounding surprised at all.

"Absolutely," I responded, my voice conveying concern.

"James Thompson to the nurse station." The voice said again, sounding angry.

"I should probably go see what the nurse needs," I said, though a nagging feeling of unease lingered; I quickly added, "keep your eyes peeled, and whatever you do, stay out of sight."

"You can trust us!" Josh could only say, not sounding convinced.

"I know I can, and I'm glad I have friends like all of you to help me." I said, as I was leaving for the nurse's station.

The moment I turned the corner, I approached the nurse's office. Nurse Yvonne was in a position of authority; there she was, holding an envelope, a wicked grin plastered across her face.

"About time," she said as I arrived at the desk. "I need you to deliver this urgently to Ian's Peak Laboratory."

"Ian's Peak Laboratory, but that's on the other side of town!" I said, not sounding too pleased.

"You've got a problem with that?" the evil-looking nurse asked. "it won't take you long on your bike."

"No!" I said, "I haven't got a problem with that."

Despite my apprehension about cycling across town today. I concluded that if this Nurse is behind all of this, she'd want me out of the way to prevent me from interfering with her scheme. As I rode away from the hospital on my bicycle, I pulled out my mobile and immediately contacted Josh.

"Hey James, what's up?" Josh curiously asked.

"I have to do an errand for the nurse on the other side of town," I said. "Would you and Zac be okay with everything."

"Everything is fine here, James," Josh said. "quickly complete that job and come back."

I went quiet for a second, and Josh looked at his phone to see if I was still on the other end and realised it was still going.

"Are you still there, James?" Josh wanted to know.

"Yeah, I'm still here," I said, "but….."

"But… what?" Josh questioned, "What aren't you telling me?"

"I suspect the nurse wanted me out of the way," I said.

"You think that she knows something?" Josh asked.

"Yeah, I do," I said.

"What did she want you to deliver?" Josh questioned.

"An envelope; not sure if it's real, though." I replied.

"Why don't you open it and see?" Josh suggested.

"Just wait," I said. "I'll open it right now while you're on the phone."

I opened the envelope. I couldn't believe what was inside, just some shredded newspaper and nothing else. I was right; the Nurse wanted me out of the way so her plans would work, which meant my friends could be in danger.

"I was right," I said over the phone. "it was just some newspaper that was shredded up."

"Oh really," said the voice over the phone. The voice wasn't any of my friends. It was a voice I recognised from all the time I worked at the hospital. It was the voice of Nurse Yvonne.

"What have you done with Josh?" I wanted to know.

"You don't have to worry about your little friends." Yvonne said, "You are not going to ruin my plans."

"You leave them alone!" I demanded.

"What would you do on your own?" Yvonne said, laughing hard over the phone.

"I will destroy you," I said. "your day will surely be ruined."

"I have put your friends in a dark place that you will never get to them. It's a place you are familiar with, but not from this century, and they will soon be sacrificed to the almighty beast himself." She said as the phone cut off.

I'm more than ready to find my friends. Nurse Yvonne has kept them captive, and I will stop her wicked ten-year plan.

Given the temporary unavailability of my friends, rescuing them now falls completely to me. Her statement, 'It's a place you are familiar with, but not from this century,' left me pondering its exact meaning, the puzzling implication prompting a need for further understanding of her cryptic message.

Chapter Seven

Before entering the elevator, we efficiently organised our belongings to ensure we had everything. My friends are missing, and their safety is causing me serious concern. Why didn't I foresee that? Their support has been essential in preparing me for this journey, and I'm excited and ready to start this adventure because of them.

I am essential to this operation's success. I sincerely hope that the fact of Zac's existence, and his considerable influence, remains completely unknown to Yvonne. The story I have uncovered involves the enigmatic man who will vanish, and his mysterious relationships with Yvonne and the year 1860. As the great-great-grandson of Ian Peak, the town's founder, Stuart Peak was a respected figure, his lineage clear in his strong jawline and piercing gaze that reflected generations of Peaks. Stuart is Zac's uncle. Perhaps Yvonne was jealous of the city's namesake.

Because of the connection between Stuart and Ian Peak, and because of the puzzling nature of Stuart's disappearance, it is necessary to investigate Yvonne's potential involvement and rule out the possibility of coincidence. Much later, I discovered the surprising truth that the woman he was visiting, a woman named Linda Peak, was in fact his mum. His dad, whom she married four decades prior, mysteriously vanished, leaving no clue as to his whereabout. I'm understanding the situation better. Unraveling the mystery of the town's 1860s history and the peculiar events of every year on November 18th, this just add a dimension to the intrigue. I plan to conquer the wicked nurse and banish her to hell. I constantly reflect on how I'll manage everything alone, with no help.

My next vision involves my friends, who appear cold and are being held captive, a scene that fills me with unease. Sadly, the Christmas bracelet, a present from me to Sam, slipped off her wrist. Losing the item went unnoticed by her; she was entirely unaware she had dropped it at all.

The resemblance to Cave Death is uncanny, a fact that is simply impossible given my eyewitness account of the cave's demolition earlier this year.

Chapter Eight

My curiosity about what remained in Cave Death drove me to investigate and explore its depths. Only rubble and dust remained after the destruction of the cave. Why did my dream feature my friends in a dark cave? A terrifying darkness surrounded them. I tried to get inside the cave rubble. Something on the ground caught my attention. I reached down and picked the item up. It was the bracelet that I bought Sam for Christmas. That's not possible; it appeared to have been buried for centuries. After everything I've been through, nothing seems to be impossible. Therefore, the Cave Death event must date back to 1860, not the present day. There's no way I can rescue them from a different time period. I couldn't stop thinking about my friends all night; eventually, I fell fast asleep.

****

Still reeling from the unbelievable events of the previous night, witnessed while everyone else slept soundly, Ian Peak awoke at camp the following morning in a state of utter disbelief, his mind struggling to process what he had seen. If one were to have witnessed Yvonne's shocking behavior and the underlying reasons for her presence at the camp, they would find it absolutely unbelievable. Ian wanted to share his bizarre, unbelievable story. He kept it a secret, the loneliness overwhelming as he questioned whether anyone would believe his story. What was the horrific sight he witnessed, a monstrous being rising from the earth and carrying away the corpses of those dear to him? The doctor recalled reading that in the Bible at church, but this wasn't church, nor was it biblical.

***

Back at camp that night, Dr. Ian Peak tossed and turned, knowing the Nurse would again deceive those loyal and lovely people. Ian couldn't sleep; his eyes were wide, he was drinking more coffee, and a terrifying suspense gripped him. What would Yvonne do next, and was he next to be thrown to the beast?

The next morning, after a night of troubled sleep, Ian Peak realised he had a huge amount of work to do; he needed to find out what was going on in his small, and ever-shrinking community, and, most significantly, why. He avoided crowds because he could not respond to their inquiries. Dr. Ian Peak was running out of time; therefore, he urgently needed to find out Yvonne's actions to prevent any unforeseen consequences.

Nurse Yvonne walked into the room where Dr. Ian Peak was already present.

"What's wrong?" she wanted to know, "you seemed quiet today."

The Doctor could not provide her with an answer and avoided direct eye contact. Rather than acknowledging her presence, his eyes moved past her, as if he were addressing someone situated directly behind her.

"Nothing." He could only say, choking on his words.

She looked deeply at him to see if she could read him like a book.

"I know you were there early this morning. I saw you." She seemed to be cold and cruel, and that was something that worried Ian.

95

Once the nurse had exited the tent, leaving Ian Peak to his reflections, he promptly produced a book hidden under his bed, located a particular page within what appeared to be his journal, and recorded his thoughts on an empty page.

16th of November 1860

My worry and concern is growing regarding the people in my charge and their current situation, and I want to ensure their safety. My suspicions regarding Nurse Yvonne increasingly felt less like a figment of my imagination and more like a grim reality, solidifying with each passing moment. I, Ian Peak, am still reeling from the unbelievable events I witnessed last night on the fifteenth; an experience so extraordinary that even I have difficulty believing it, making me skeptical that others would accept my account as truth. In a disturbing ritual, Yvonne has been given the discarded remains of these humans as nourishment to the Devil that lives in the underworld. My investigation continues; I'm still seeking further details about this nurse and her proposed actions. The woman's pregnancy is advancing at an astonishing pace, showing a considerable increase in size daily; just the other day, her pregnancy was only recently noticeable, but now, surprisingly, the baby appears ready to be born soon. I have absolutely no idea what is happening, but I can tell you that there is some unusual activity going on at the camp.

I am signing off from my work for the day.

Ian Peak - 1860

Exhausted, Dr. Ian Peak eventually fell into a deep sleep; however, a strange and mysterious situation was developing in the camp, completely unnoticed by him. Nurse Yvonne departed the Centre, this time for a faraway place. It was a mysterious cave into which she cautiously entered. For over a day, Yvonne held Sam, Josh, and Zac captive within the confines of the cave, preventing their escape.

"What do you want from us?" Sam asked.

"I want to know what James' plans are?" the nurse questioned.

"We have no idea what you talking about!" Zac said, sounding concerned.

"If you don't tell me, I will feed you and your little friends to the Devil that lives underground."

"The Devil!" Zac said, sounding more nervous than before.

"I know who you are, Zachary Peak." The Nurse said,

"So, you know my name, big deal." Zac replied.

"It is a big deal because you are related to Dr Ian Peak. I may feed you to the devil anyway." She said with a sneaky grin.

"Over my dead body!" Sam exclaimed, then realised her mistake.

"That goes double for me," Josh said.

My alarm went off, and I woke up without knowing what would happen next in the dream. Now he knows precisely what Yvonne was up to all those years ago, and she also knows who Zac is and that he's related to the founder of this town. I better get there soon; it may be too late for Zac.

I got up and went straight to the desk early in the morning, where the Professor's journal was. I picked up the journal, opened the page to the book's last entry, or what I thought was the previous entry, and noticed a new one.

The journal entry begins, "Good morning, James. I presume you've just had another dream or vision from 1860. Your discovery revealed your friends' capture in a cave in 1860, later called Cave Death. Knowing you've figured it out, it's clear you aim to save your friends from 1860. I'm about to tell you something about The Basement; when you enter the elevator, you will be taken to a dark place, but there is a portal, which is a wormhole down there to take you to the year 1860, and you will rescue your friends and destroy Yvonne, the Devil and the basement. You don't have long, though. You only have about 3 hours; once time is up and you are not through the portal back to your year, then I'm afraid you will all be stuck in 1860."

'What if I failed?' I asked myself, '1860 would become our permanent home.'

I would have to wait around for Professor Lynx to create this experiment. I got to succeed and beat this thing.

***

I'm working my regular shift at 3 pm. Everything seemed so normal; Nurse Yvonne was at the desk with her evil grin when she looked straight at me. Do the others who worked with her have any idea what she's up to? My backpack contains everything, which hides in the elevator, ready to go. I am prepared for whatever will happen. I'm sad that Josh wouldn't be beside me in the basement; it would have been much better. I'm sure that time is slowing down today, which wouldn't surprise me. I want to get things moving a little faster, so I can get it over and done with. While moping the floor, I had another vision.

Chapter Nine

The three waited in the dark cave, uncertain. Zack strolled over to Josh, who was sitting down.

"I'm curious about her comment that she knew who I was." Zac said, sounding concerned.

"I'm sure it's because you are a Peak."

"What's that got to do with it?" Zac wanted to know.

"Yvonne had it in for the Peak family since the 1860s."

"In other words, I could be in deep shit?"

"Don't worry," Sam said, sounding reassuring, "We won't let anything happen to you."

"Yeah, don't forget that your dad disappeared all those years ago, and now your uncle suppose to be disappearing soon."

"We might not be with James," Sam said, "but we'll need to work out a way of helping him."

"Do you know where we are?" Zac asked,

"Not completely sure. Has anyone noticed what the nurse Yvonne is wearing?"

"I have," Sam Said,

"Zac, I don't think we are in the 21st century!" Josh stated.

"What do you mean?" Zac wanted to know.

"I think we are in the 19th century,"

"How do you know?" Sam asked.

"As I was reading about the history of Ian's Peak, I came across some photos of the original nurses' uniforms from when the hospital was first built, and the uniform that this nurse was wearing was identical to those in the pictures."

"Are you telling me that we are not only being kidnapped," Zac said, "But we have been taken to a time, centuries before any of us was born."

"I couldn't have put it better myself." Josh said,

"That's incredible." Sam replied, not sounding too pleased. "It's a pity we can't let James know what's going on and where we are."

"There is a way." Josh Said,

"How?" Zac wanted to know.

"We can write to him."

"What a great idea, and then we can post it at our nearest Post Box!" Sam replied, sounding sarcastic.

"Nah, but if we write a note and bury it somewhere that we think James could find it."

"Oh, I see now; so in our future, James can find the note?" Sam questioned, "I think you've been watching Back to the Future once too often."

***

I shook off the vision of my friends in the 19th century. What will happen to them? I need to find this note that they left for me to find, and it may give me some idea of how they are doing and what was going on all those years ago.

Chapter Ten

The elevator remains stubbornly still, and I'm left standing here at 6:50, my patience wearing thin as I wait. I received a note from my friends earlier today, and I wasn't surprised to see its 19th-century date. A note lay hidden within the cave's rubble all these years. The information presented contained nothing new or insightful that I wasn't already familiar with.

I made a sign that reads 'out of order' and placed it in front of the elevator to let people know that it's not working. From my position, I can feel the sense of the motion of the elevator as it moves, a quiet rhythmic shift that makes itself known to me even though I am standing still within its confines. In a fortunate turn of events, orchestrated by destiny itself, the elevator doors opened on the very floor where Stuart Peak was expected. I peered outside and there stood Stuart, unmistakably wearing the outfit from my vivid dream, the one where he would find himself inside this elevator.

"Sorry," I said, "Out of order."

"Okay," Stuart replied, "I catch the next one."

It didn't seem to bother Stuart as if he knew this elevator would take him to a darkened place in the hospital called the basement.

The elevator doors closed, the metallic clang a stark counterpoint to the frantic hammering of my heart, which sped up to a pace far exceeding its previous rhythm. Because the momentum was too great for me to maintain my grasp, I fell to the ground just as Stuart had done in my dream. With my eyes squeezed shut for the duration of the descent, I didn't open them until a heavy thud signaled that my journey downwards had concluded.

I paused for a moment to collect my thoughts, taking in my surroundings to confirm that the elevator had finally ceased its movement. It appeared the elevator had stopped. I was getting up when the elevator jerked, making me fall. I slowly stood, the elevator doors sliding open in front of me. Heavy darkness cloaked the area, including the outside. It was pitch black. I am standing here, much like I envisioned Stuart would stand in my dreams. Because of my actions, I could prevent him from suffering certain harm, and I feel relieved knowing that he is now safe and sound.

***

Only then did I remember the journal I'd been carrying. The map of the portal's location gives me the power to rescue my friends from the past. From my vantage point in the basement, I could see the creature in the distance, though it was quite far away. Fire surrounded the beast, creating an image that made me feel as if I were in hell itself. The creature before me is none other than the devil, and I find myself in a terrible confrontation. I need to leave before he sees me. The devil, breathing fire, approaches. Running as fast as my legs would carry me, I could hear the distinct sound of his footsteps pursuing me from behind, and when I glanced back, I saw the creature desperately trying to close the distance between me. I lost my footing and took a hard fall onto the unforgiving ground. The fire was hotter than Ian's Peak's hottest day.

Having finally found a place where I could hide, I then stood up again. In the grip of terror, I closed my eyes, my silent prayer a desperate plea that this creature, whatever it was, would remain unaware of my presence. I don't understand how I could destroy this creature because of its size. Only when the creature was a safe distance away did I take the time to open my backpack carefully and find the page I needed. Once again, I read the words of Professor Lynx: "The image shows what seems to be either a portal, or perhaps a wormhole, a theoretical tunnel through space and time. Famous scientist Albert Einstein came up with the idea of wormholes in the early 1900s, a theory that has fascinated many people. I have to admit, in retrospect, that he was correct in his judgment. Einstein was born in 1879, that would make him 12 in my time, but he wasn't born in the year that you will be entering. Just remember to be careful entering the wormhole; it can be overwhelming. I'm sure, James, that you can handle it. Good Luck–Signing of–Professor C.T. Lynx."

I examined the map and diagram, comparing the two to pinpoint the location of the wormhole. As I traced the route showed on the map, I encountered a large, heavy door which blocked my further progress. While scrutinizing the door, a chilling inscription immediately came into view: 'Enter at your own risk,' It appears as though there is some sort of interference preventing my entry. I'm certain that a way to pass through the door must be discovered. My memory drifted back years ago, to a time when we had ventured into the perilous depths of what we called Cave Death, and Josh found the button that opened the door. I searched high and low for something similar that may open the door. I could not find any tool or device that would successfully open it.

The Professor's journal showed how to open the door. The map showed a lever was located to the right-hand side. I went to the spot where the map showed where the lever should be, and what I found instead was a hole filled to the brim with cobwebs. The hole appeared unused for years; its rusted metal showed significant age and decay. My first action was to clear away the cobweb from the hole's entrance; afterwards, I proceeded to cautiously insert my hand into the hole to find and touch the lever. I could clearly hear the loud whooshing sound from inside the room. Given the complex circumstances of this matter, I find myself curious as to the identity or nature of the unknown element in question. Seeing the wormhole in the room proved Albert Einstein's theories correct. Every single detail I have presented is entirely accurate, and I possess comprehensive documentation to substantiate each claim. Because none of my friends would remember the forthcoming events, I'm not able to share any information about it with them.

Now I'm in the room looking straight at the whirling wormhole, hoping that this would work and that I would turn up in the 19th century. What would happen if this doesn't work out? 'Here goes nothing!' I thought to myself.

I ran towards the wormhole and jumped right into the centre; a strange feeling came over me while going through.

Chapter Eleven

My eyes fluttered open gradually, a peculiar sensation of displacement creeping in as I attempted to make sense of the strange environment around me. As far as the eye can see, in every direction where I stand, there are lush and vibrant forests. The tree prevented me from falling farther; otherwise, I would have struck it. In the far distance, I could hear the distinct sound of someone running. I have always dreamed of going back in time and experiencing the year 1860 firsthand. Is that possible? Raising myself to a sitting position, I then looked upwards, my gaze searching. My calculations suggest, if they are correct, that the cave, later to be called Cave Death, lies to the far west. I attempted to stand, but I couldn't maintain my balance. I promptly collapsed to the floor once more. The journey had a far more effect on me than I acknowledged, leaving a lasting impression. As I stood up, I paused for a few minutes in the same spot, collecting my thoughts before proceeding carefully to where I believed the cave is located. The moon's soft glow provided enough light for me to find my way to the cave successfully, even though the night was darker than expected. As the sound of approaching footsteps grew louder, fear propelled me to seek cover behind some nearby bushes, where I stood perfectly still, my breath suspended in my chest. When I initially looked around, there was no one in sight. So that's the proof

I needed. The setting is the 19th century; but I wonder if the specific time period is, indeed, the 1860s.

Two men came into view, strolling and then pausing close by.

"We need to get this Charles, he's evil," one guy said.

"We sure do," said the other guy, "claiming that he can see events that haven't happened yet."

"Once we capture him, we meed to hang him."

I was completely astonished and utterly shocked by the information I had just received. Who's the target of 'Getting Hanged?'

When they have gone, I am making my way towards the cave.

I see the cave ahead. I recognised it, same as ever. I recalled Josh falling into a ditch. Remembering the rope, I carefully and slowly used it to lower myself down. If my memory serves me correctly, Josh unfortunately sprained his ankle after a fall, despite the incident not being too far in the past. As I stood there, noises from the area ahead of my current location were clear. Upon seeing a torch on the cave wall, one similar to the ones the men themselves carried, the men concluded another person had been in the cave, or that they were not alone. The only individual I know to have been familiar with the cave during the 1860s was Nurse Yvonne, and I can't say with certainty if there were others. Could this be the year of the settlement in my dream, or could it be another year?

From my past visits, the cave's structure came back to me. I could hear some noise up ahead; could it be my friends? Drawn by the noise, I found a lit room, Professor Lynx's office, where his journal held our conversations across centuries. Instead of my friends, I found an older gentleman with a lengthy beard writing in an enormous book upon entering the room. Startled by the noise I made on arrival, the man spun around.

"Ahh, James Thompson," said the strange-looking man.

I then recognised who it was. It turned out to be Professor Lynx. He looks older than 30.

"Professor Lynx?" I could only say,

"I was expecting you." He said.

"Why am I here? I'm meant to be in the 1860s," I declared.

"Yes, there is a reason for it." The professor said, "First thing, you can't run around in 1860 dress like that. I have some clothes for you to wear, and you must take some for your friends, too."

Professor Lynx gave me a bundle of clothes that the townsfolk would have worn in the 1860s, attracting no one's attention.

"There is also something else you need to know," Said Professor Lynx.

"What's that?" I wanted to know.

"Be careful," the professor warned. "Your major priority is the baby's safety and well-being."

"You talking about Nurse Yvonne's babe?"

"Yes," the professor said, "If something happens to him, then everything will change and not for the better."

"Why?" I said, "Who is the baby? What did he become?"

"I need to show you what will happen if the baby dies."

"How?"

"I will show you another secret that comes with the powers you gain."

"What's that?" I asked, now sounding more curious than ever.

Close your eyes and concentrate. Think of Yvonne and the baby. Consider a past scenario with the baby, then imagine an alternate future after he dies.

***

In my mind's eye, we're fighting Yvonne and the devil in an 1860s basement. I see Josh, Sam, and Zac at the corner where Yvonne sacrificed humans to the beast. They wore the clothes Professor Lynx gave me. I can't see myself in the vision and wonder what happened. Zac walked toward the Devil's hole.

Yvonne saw, in my vision, that Zac was related to Ian Peak. He's going to be in trouble. I arrived on time with their clothes. I just had a look and saw myself in the picture, right behind Yvonne. Is this the only method available to prevent further sacrifices on her part and to safeguard Ian's Peak from future catastrophes? In the vision, I followed Yvonne from behind and then pushed her into the hole. Yvonne screamed as the Devil's fiery breath sent her flying upward, and she fell back toward him. As Yvonne falls, the Devil's mouth snaps shut at her, taking Yvonne down below with him.

As the Devil's mouth snapped shut, I successfully gave the Devil holy water. As the mouth closes on her, Yvonne's bones continue to crunch. I got everyone down for cover. A loud explosion shook us; rocks fell everywhere. I survey my surroundings when the coast is clear. The hole had disappeared. The explosion destroyed the Devil, Yvonne, and the basement. No baby, either. *Professor Lynx said the baby's survival affects the future. I wonder what would have changed if we had destroyed the basement as I saw it. My vision jolted back to the Cave Death moment during our cave exploration, completely out of the blue. Everything up to a certain point happened the way it happened.*

109

Josh fell in the hole and sprained his ankle. I found something to support him, so he can continue exploring the cave with me. The room that had the experiment no longer existed. The cave differed from our expectations. I gained no powers. Last year's vision involved Wayne and Young Paul's kidnapping. We couldn't find Paul without the powers. The cave exploded. Three funerals appeared in the vision. Who was the third gasket between Lindsay Peterson and Paul Brown? Then I realised it was Mum. The baby's death in 1860 change the future for the worst.

I opened my eyes, seeing Professor Lynx.

"It's you," I said, after a few minutes. "You're the baby from 1860; that explains how you know about building this experiment."

"You see if the baby gets destroyed in the crossfire, then everything will change, and you and Josh will lose someone last year."

"Then I better not fail this, mission. I need to destroy the devil and the basement separate from the nurse."

I could hear people outside trying to get into the cave.

"Quick," Professor Lynx said, "You must go."

"What's going to happen to you?" I asked,

"You already know what's going to happen,"

"Is there anything I can do to help?"

"No, just go and James, good luck.

Chapter Twelve

I open my eyes to a different time. Perhaps it's 1860 this time. I felt queasy; and slowly looked around the area. I heard of Jet Lag; what would you call it when you move through time? Time Lag! This feels strange. I slowly rise once the dizziness passes. Regrouping, I continued the mission. I finally got up. I knew my location and where the cave is situated. This is worse than I thought; I have to ensure no harm to Yvonne's baby. That is something that I need my friends to help me with. I am heading now towards the cave.

I used my usual route into the cave. Through the hole. Someone had already mounted a torch on the wall. It did not require a significant amount of time for Nurse Yvonne to organise and prepare the cave. With a torch in hand, I set off toward the professor's office, beginning my walk down the corridor. During my walk in that direction, another vision unexpectedly and surprisingly came into my mind.

We were all standing near the hole; it looked like Zac was near it and ready to be pushed in by Yvonne. I tried to distract her, so she would forget about Zac being there. Yvonne was in pain, and she fell to the ground in agony. I moved Zac away from the hole next to Sam and Josh. Yvonne was on the ground, ripping off her clothes. Something was coming out of her, and it was her baby being born!

The vision vanished as quickly as it appeared. I have a plan. Once the baby is born, we'll demolish Yvonne, the devil, and the basement.

I went to the room where my friends were imprisoned. Years ago, upon our initial discovery of the perilous Cave Death, we made our first attempt to enter this very room. Somewhere, a button awaits to be pushed; my first assumption was that Professor Lynx had wired it, a notion I later discovered to be inaccurate. As I walked, I distinctly heard footsteps following closely behind me. The footsteps continued. Yvonne's considerable size made it quite apparent that she was very pregnant and on the verge of giving birth. I observed her entrance. Opening the door, she pressed a button. Thirty years passed between the button and the experiment. Unbelievable! Yvonne initially placed the button in the cave, which her son later used in his invention. Muffled voices were coming from the room. Yvonne shoved Zac ahead of her.

"What do you want from me?" Zac screamed out.

Zac fell when Yvonne pushed him. As Zac fell, he looked at me. I signaled for him to be quiet. Zac stood without speaking. Yvonne pushed him towards the exit. After Yvonne left, I pressed the button. Unexpectedly, Josh saw his best friend, not Yvonne.

"James," Josh said,

Sam came up to me and hugged me, but didn't want to let me go. I don't blame her. She must have been through a lot.

"Hey, I'm here now," James said. "We're going to get out of this, but first, put these on."

Having received the clothes from James, both Sam and Josh quickly took hold of them.

"What!" Sam said. "It looks like some old piece of cloth."

"That's what they wore in the 19th Century,"

They put on their 19th-century clothes. Josh notice James looked concerned.

"What is it, James?" Josh questioned.

"There is something that we have to be careful about."

"What's that?" Josh wanted to know.

"The baby that Yvonne is carrying,"

"What about it?" Sam questioned.

"We need to make sure that he's safe and not being destroyed along with Yvonne,"

"Why?" Josh asked curiously.

"How bad will it be if something happens to him?" Sam asked.

"I've foreseen the alternate future should Yvonne's baby die," I stated. "It will jeopardise everything,"

"Why?" Josh asked, "Who did he become?"

"He's Professor Lynx; he was adopted from a Lynx at the camp. If the baby doesn't make it, when we discovered the cave, there be an empty room and no experiments. I wouldn't get the power of Dream Reality. It also means that we didn't find your brother in time. If you remember, my powers found him. It also means that the explosion of the Cave, would have been more than a blood bath."

"Holly shit," Josh could only say, "It looks like we better save the kid then."

"That's the plan," I replied. "We better get going before it's too late for Zac."

***

From our hidden position behind the bushes, we are keeping a close watch on Yvonne and Zac. It appears that the day is done and the night is setting in as the last rays of sunlight fade away. We didn't want to attract attention, so we chose to leave the torch where it was.

"What are you kids doing," a voice said, that came from behing us.

When I turned around, it was Dr. Ian Peak.

"What are you kids doing away from the camp,"

"We were following the nurse."

"You know about all this?" Dr. Ian Peak questioned.

"Yes," I said.

"Hang about," Ian Peak said. "I don't remember seeing you at the camp. Who are you?"

"I can't tell you now," I said. "The nurse has our friend up there; we need to get him."

Dr. Ian Peak looked over and saw Zac tied up with Yvonne.

"What is she going to do with him," Dr. Ian Peak said,

"She's going to sacrifice him to the Devil," I replied,

"There is something seriously wrong here," said Dr. Ian Peak. "For one thing, he's not dead, and for another thing, he's only a kid. The ones she sacrificed were men who passed away."

"There is a reason for it, though," I said, not knowing how to explain everything to the Doctor.

"What's that?" Dr. Ian Peak asked,

"It's a long story," I said.

"You kids showed up out of nowhere; your friend is going to be sacrificed, nothing here tonight make any sense and you said that it's a long story."

"It sounds bizarre, I know, and the full story might sound crazy," I said, trying to sound convincing.

"I enjoy hearing it; I have seen a lot of weird things in the last few days, and nothing else would shock me."

"See that kid up there; his name is Zac Peak. He will be your great-grandson in many years to come," I said,

"What are you trying to tell me?" Dr. Ian Peak looked confused.

"No easy way of putting it," I could only say. "We are from another time and came from the future. We had to come here to stop Yvonne from doing what she is doing!"

"That's impossible," Dr. Ian's Peak said. "We all know no one can go back in time."

"Well, we are the proof that it's possible, and you've never seen us before in the camp. So how would you explain that?" I said, trying to convince the Doctor.

"I guess so," Dr. Ian Peak said, unsure and confused.

"We haven't got much time; we have to save your grandson, Zac," Josh said.

"You're right. We need to save him before it's too late," said Ian Peak.

"We'll need to destroy Yvonne without harming her unborn child," I said.

"How are we going to do that?" Sam curiously asked,

"According to Professor Lynx," I said, "we need some of this brew he gave me; he made it especially to destroy the beast that lives underground."

"Did you see the Professor?" Josh curiously asked,

"Before I manage to get to this time, the wormhole took me to 1892, just after Professor Lynx created the Laboratory, and just on the same day that the people hanged him."

"Professor Lynx," said Ian Peak. "He's not related to Jenkin Lynx by any chance,"

I couldn't answer, despite knowing the answer. Telling Ian Peak the truth risks the future.

"Come on, we got to do this now," I said, sounding more worried.

"What is it, James?" Sam questioned. "What aren't you telling us?"

"Sam, we only have a few hours to do this and go home."

"What would happen if we don't do it in a few hours?" Josh wanted to know.

"The wormhole will close, and we will be stuck in 1860 forever."

"Then what are we waiting for?" Josh said, "I don't want to end up in the history books."

"What's going on here?" A voice said from behind us.

When they turned around, they noticed a man standing there; I had seen him many times in my dream. It was Jenkins Lynx. I know in my dream he saved Yvonne's baby and adopted him as his own.

"I repeat, what's going on here?" Jenkins said again, "Who are you three? I don't remember seeing you at camp?"

"It's a long story, Jenkins," Dr. Ian Peak said. "I will explain it to you the best I can."

I was standing behind the nurse. There is a certain characteristic about her that stands out.

Remaining within my line of sight, Zak's expression is one of sheer terror, and his desperate pleas seem for someone to save him from the horrifying experience he's currently suffering through. As I arrived, a look of undeniable pleasure spread across his face, a clear sign he had been eagerly awaiting our presence. The unfolding events received an explanation from Dr. Ian Peak, who, along with Jenkins, was absent; however, I believe this explanation was doomed to fail because of Jenkins' anticipated skepticism and his lack of comprehension regarding the circumstances. Considering that even if I had lived in the 1860s and spun a fantastical yarn about time travel, I find it hard to believe that such a tale would have been believable even to myself. Sam, Josh, and I bear the responsibility of rescuing Zac from the beast in the basement, and we must do so without jeopardising the safety of the expectant mother and her unborn child. I will tend to the nurse, and Josh will apply Professor Lynx's potion to deal with the devil that is found in the depths below.

I had a premonition about what was going to happen in the next few minutes. According to the vision, Josh poured the potion on the beast and fell back; simultaneously, the beast came out of the hole screaming and pushing Yvonne, snapped at Yvonne and pulled her down the hole with the beast. Immediately after that, a baby's cry, sharp and piercing, sliced through the air and filled my ears with its insistent sound. Because baby Professor Lynx survived, the plan remains unchanged; we will venture into the cave and the discover of the experiment.

I saw Josh pour the potion down the beast's hole. Just as foreseen, the beast seized Yvonne.

Epilogue

I woke to morning light streaming through my window. How did I get here? I last remember 1860. We rescued my friends and then conquered the evil nurse and the basement. I did, however, remember something else about Jenkins Lynx.

Distracted, Yvonne didn't see the beast rising from the depths of the earth until it was too late, consuming her in a single, horrific instant that ended her life. The beast and the basement were destroyed in a catastrophic event, leaving both in ruins—a fitting end for such a terrible creature. A hole, a noticeable gap in the earth's surface, was present. A baby's cry, weak and thin, reached my ears from the depths of the hole. From the hole, Jenkins rescued the baby. The man understood that the infant represented Yvonne's sole remaining possession, a poignant reminder of what she had lost. Despite the devastation caused by Yvonne, her baby persevered and lived.

"Charles Thomas Lynx, that's what I shall name him." Jenkins said, sounding please with himself.

I still remember that day vividly. His neck bore a birthmark shaped like Ian's Peak. That mark looked familiar to me, and I recalled having seen it somewhere previously. Early this year's events came flooding back to me; I recalled the time Professor Lynx had rescued my mum from the deadly depths of Cave Death. Try to remember the birthmark that belonged to that well-respected and elderly professor. I recognised it immediately; it was undoubtedly the same birthmark. A smile touched my lips as the identity of Yvonne's baby finally dawned

***

I was lying in bed and still thinking about everything in 1860. "James," Mum said, "Your phone has been ringing nonstop this morning."

I couldn't help but think, what have I changed in this world? I have gone back in time, and things could change. Did Josh go into Cave Death with me? Have I ever met Sam?

I grabbed my phone from the lounge and called Josh.

"Hey Josh, how are you?" I said, "Wasn't the mission exciting?"

"What mission?" Josh questioned,

My past basement destruction meant my friends wouldn't remember Professor Lynx's words.

"Oh, never mind." I said, "I'm going to give Zac a call; I meet you at the park."

"OK, James, see you then."

I rang Zac, to invite him to the park with us, his phone rang. a childish voice answered.

"Hi, Zac speaking," the voice said.

"Hi Zac, it's James," I said. "Josh and I am going to the park. Do you want to join us?"

"I can't, James. My dad promised to take me fishing today."

120

"Your Dad, but he's ….." I couldn't finish the sentence.

"He's what James," Zac said,

"Never mind, Zac, that's great. Have a great fishing trip."

"Thanks."

I couldn't believe I had changed the past and improved the future.

Ten years before the current time, Zac and his mum stood patiently waiting for the elevator to arrive. From the place where Zac's dad had emerged, Zac enthusiastically leaped into his dad's embracing arms. I was very pleased and relieved that things worked out so well in the end for Zac, resulting in a joyful reunion with his dad. Following the destruction, my thoughts briefly drifted back to the year 1860, conjuring a fleeting image of that time.

A remarkably short time saw the complete recovery of everyone at the camp who had been reported sick, including my great-grandfather. And then, a completely new and unexpected vision materialised, offering a different perspective.

***

Despite the clear sign that the building in the dream was a hospital, its structure and features bore no resemblance to Ian's Peak Hospital, my place of work, which was a stark contrast to what I expected. While the structure outwardly resembled a private hospital situated somewhere within the city limits, its precise location remained elusive, and even its function as a hospital was shrouded in uncertainty, making definitive identification a challenging task. Taking into account the visible clues such as the atmosphere and the overall feel of the place, this was a hospital that specialised in the care of mothers and newborns. As a doctor at the end of the operating table watched intently, his eyes fixed on the area where the baby was expected, the sounds of a woman's anguished screams echoed through the room, a stark counterpoint to the anticipation of the impending birth. This woman was in more pain and agony than she had ever been in before, even more than during her two previous childbirths. Because of her own experience of going through labor, she developed a comprehensive and intimate understanding of what labor pains truly feel like.

Surrounding the area there were lights that were flickering on and off, creating an eerie and unsettling atmosphere. With the Doctor concentrating his full attention on the immediate task at hand, which involved a poor woman in immense pain delivering a child, the unfolding scene left one to ponder the many outcomes. As the pain continued, the nurse held the patient's hand, allowing for light squeezes of comfort; however, unexpectedly, the patient's grip was so strong that her fingernail pierced his hand. His scream was louder than the woman's on the table, a sound that surpassed even her cries. With the woman in obvious pain on the operating table, the Doctor was nearly as preoccupied with the hazard of the broken glass spread across the operating room floor, a significant safety concern adding to the already stressful situation.

"Calm down," The Doctor said to the woman, "hopefully it won't be too long before your child arrives out into this strange world."

Because of the intense pain she was experiencing, the woman's efforts to soothe herself were unsuccessful. He asserted an affair was the reason for his suspicions, beginning around the time of their youngest child's birth and based on the idea of the child's paternity. That she hadn't had sex with her husband or anyone else further puzzled her. The situation was unusual, yet she found herself unable to persuade her husband of this strange and unsettling truth.

Leaning over, the Doctor urges her to push, and she does. He can now see the head of her child.

"He's almost here," the Doctor said, "keep pushing."

As if a child were playing with the switches, the light inside the theatre flickered on and off.

Pushing with all her might, the woman at the table continued her efforts. The Doctor couldn't believe what he had seen. His mouth just opened, and he screamed ...

The Dream continues ....

THE DARK SECRET OF
IAN'S PEAK
BOOK TWO
TWO CURSES. ONE BOY WHO CAN SEE BEYOND REALITY.
D.J. BRAND

Part Three: *Déjà Vu*

Henry Van Dyke has lived his life more times than anyone should. To the outside world he's a cheerful, ordinary boy, but on his fourteenth birthday he dies—only to awaken again on the day he was born. Trapped in an endless loop forged by a powerful curse placed on his mother long before he existed, Henry is forced to relive the same life over and over. Desperate to save him, Kylie Van Dyke turns to James Thompson, the only student at Ian's Peak High with the rare ability to enter Dream Reality. If anyone can unravel the *Déjà Vu* curse and free Henry from his repeating fate, it's James… but every reset tightens the clock.

Part Four: *The Curse of Slimy Slim*

A century-old pirate play returns to the stage—and with it, a mystery no one expects. During the performance, the actor playing Slimy Slim vanishes before the audience's eyes. Most believe it's part of the show… everyone except James, who has already witnessed the disappearance in a Dream Reality vision. His search for answers pulls him into a dangerous multiverse filled with pirates, crocodiles, and the restless ghosts of every performer who ever played the role. With Sam, Josh, Paul, and the cryptic clues hidden in Professor Lynx's journal, James steps into the role of Slimy Slim himself, risking everything to uncover the truth behind the cursed play.

About the Author

D.J. Brand was born and raised in Perth, Western Australia. He grew up in Lynwood before moving to Northam in 1979 to complete his schooling. His passion for storytelling began early, and in the 1980s he developed the first ideas for a tale built around an experiment that grants the power of Dream Reality—allowing a boy to dream of the past, present, and future, and to solve mysteries hidden within those visions. The concept was originally shaped as a screenplay before evolving into the foundation of his book series.

Alongside his writing ambitions, he spent much of the 1980s and 1990s performing with several amateur theatre groups, including Patch Theatre, Wanneroo Limelight Theatre, and the Young Australia League Drama Academy (YALDA). His time at YALDA earned him multiple awards:

Best Actor in 1991, Over-All Excellence in 1992, and Best Actor again in both 1994 and 1995.

After completing his work with YALDA and while employed at a Perth hospital, he began writing what would become *Book One*, originally titled *Cave Death*. The book was released to the public in 2011, later receiving a new title and cover to better reflect the story and attract new readers.

From 2005 to 2010, D.J. Brand also pursued his love of music by running his own DJ business, *Cwazy D.J. 3000*. His performances spanned weddings, parties, and themed events, and he wrote and hosted a series of popular Murder Mystery Theme Nights during that time.

He hopes readers continue to enjoy the unfolding Ian's Peak series, with many more instalments planned for the future.

For more stories from Ian's Peak, visit www.djbrand.world.

Thank you for journeying into *The Dark Secret of Ian's Peak: Book One*. This story is only the beginning of the mysteries surrounding the cave, the town, and the shadows that continue to stir beneath the surface.

If you'd like to explore more stories connected to Ian's Peak, see behind-the-scenes artwork, or discover unique D.J. Brand World merchandise inspired by the series, you're welcome to visit **www.djbrand.world**.

Your support helps bring the next chapters of Ian's Peak — and many more creative projects — to life.